BITTER COLD

A STEAMPUNK SNOW QUEEN

Books and stories by Katina French

The Clockwork Republic Series
Blowhard
Big Teeth
Mirrors & Magic

The Belle Starr Series
Belle Starr: Whiskey on the Rocks
Belle Starr: The Skull Game
Belle Starr: A Pair of Aces *

The Exodus of Jerry B. Johnson
Flashes of Wonder (Collection)

Bitter Cold

(Bitter Cold is also a novella in Once Upon a Clockwork Tale)

*Coming Soon

BITTER COLD

A STEAMPUNK SNOW QUEEN

KATINA FRENCH

Per Bastet

Bitter Cold: A SteamPunk Snow Queen

Copyright © 2014 Katina French

Published by Per Bastet LLC, P.O. Box 3023 Corydon, IN 47112

Cover art by Katina French

ISBN 978-1-942166-10-8

BITTER COLD

A STEAMPUNK SNOW QUEEN

CHAPTER 1
CURIOUS CHEMISTRY

With a little luck and steady nerves, she wouldn't blow up the laboratory again.

Greta Jane Singleton stood poised over a battered wooden table covered in beakers and vials filled with mysterious liquids in a kaleidoscope of colors. A few bubbled over small oil lamps. In one corner, a dusty old grandfather clock ticked away the early morning hours. A tea tray covered with half-nibbled cucumber sandwiches and a pot of tepid tea languished on a spindly-legged table nearby.

A polished brass clockwork canary perched atop the clock, warbling a tune from The Mikado in high-pitched metallic chirps. Sunlight streamed through four windows, two on either side of a heavy wooden door and two more on the side walls of the building. The laboratory had once been the family's garden shed. After Greta nearly set the kitchen on fire with her experiments, her mother insisted she move them to the small outbuilding. Her father constantly threatened to reclaim it.

If he hadn't been terrified of the volatile substances scattered on every surface, he would probably have cleared it out ages ago. By selling some of her more practical potions and formulae, she managed to pay him a stipend for the use of the building. He still grumbled that when she burned the shed down, neither of them would have the use of it. Her earnings as an amateur alchemist would hardly pay to have a replacement built.

She worked on through the morning, mixing and heating different substances and then grinding a compound to a fine powder in a battered ceramic mortar and pestle. As the sun warmed the room, she wiped her hands on the stained and bleached apron covering her red plaid wrapper. The dress was at least twenty years out of style, but these days most fashionable dresses featured a bustle, which tended to knock things over when she turned around. She much preferred the flame-retardant wool dress, which was far more practical than the frilly frocks her mother insisted she wear when they paid calls or attended the theater.

She remained absorbed in her work, blissfully oblivious to the chaotic mess around her. It was her second attempt at creating a new alchemical formulae which she called featherfall.

If it worked, it would defy the laws of gravity. A few drops could lift a carriage a foot in the air. Applied and activated with heat, the effect could last as long as a few days. A floating carriage would require less horsepower, whether steam-generated or horse-drawn. Her best friend Kit, a mechanical genius, would be so proud of her. Between the two of them, they could create something amazing by combining her anti-gravity formulae with his machinery.

But first, she had to get the formulae to work.

Her first attempt had ended explosively. Her mother found her hiding in the pantry afterwards, her hair singed and still smoking, apron covered in vivid green splotches. Mother had been kind, although frightened, and had taken the opportunity to beg her once again to give up these foolish experiments. Alchemy was no pastime for a well-bred young lady. Greta wished her mother would finally realize she made a much better alchemist, in spite of the explosions, than she would ever make a refined young lady. If anything was a foolish waste of time in the attempt, it was the latter.

When she managed to get the featherfall to work, it would serve as proof. Maybe it would even convince her parents to let her sit for the apothecary examination.

She had good reason to hope this time she would be successful. The compound was much more finely and consistently ground. There were no distractions — with her parents off visiting relatives, there'd be no bothersome interruptions. She checked the clock. The solution mustn't simmer too long.

It's now or never.

Greta steadied her hands, lowering her protective goggles to sift the compound into a beaker.

This is where things had gone badly on her previous attempt. She held her breath. The first flecks slid into the beaker — and dissolved. She stirred it gently with a glass baton, pouring the rest into the container. The liquid turned a soft, pearlescent blue which seemed to glow. Greta exhaled in relief.

So far, so good.

❄ ❄ ❄

Her friend, Christopher "Kit" Merryweather, paced just outside. Unlike her father, his hesitation to enter the laboratory had nothing to do with any concerns about the experiment happening within. Greta was always working on some formulae; he'd grown used to their sometimes disastrous results. One accident had coated every object in the room, including Greta, with purple gelatinous goo. Another time, she had frozen the lab's contents and given herself frostbite by dropping the temperature 70 degrees.

She'd nearly given him heart failure on that occasion. A crash prompted him to run into the lab where he'd found her lying unconscious, coated in a light layer of frost. He'd carried her onto the lawn and tried to rub some warmth and color back into her hands and face. She'd sputtered awake after just a moment, only a little the worse for wear.

Although he worried, she hadn't injured herself badly. There was no use trying to talk her out of practicing alchemy. It would be like someone trying to convince him to quit tinkering with machines. They'd pursued their talents alongside each other for as long as either of them could remember, encouraging each other and sometimes working together.

Rummaging in dustbins for cogs, springs and bits of metal, Kit had been building small labor-saving devices which he sold to buy tools and more parts since he was a child. He'd taken over the carriage house behind his home as a workshop, right around the time Greta had commandeered the Singleton's garden shed.

Starting with plants from the garden and common ingredients, she'd progressed as he had, by selling basic apothecary compounds and tinctures to buy more exotic elements and supplies. Despite a few calamities, she was just as good at the alchemical sciences as he was with machinery. She just lacked his healthy sense of caution.

He raised his hand to knock on the laboratory door, then paused, struggling to find the right words. He laughed nervously. Talking to Greta was usually so easy.

She'd been his best friend since the age of five.

Their houses rested comfortably against each other in a quiet St. Louis neighborhood which shared a garden plot. Their relationship began with an argument about whether to plant vegetables or flowers. Greta had wanted roses: a rare moment of girlish behavior on her part. He conceded, fascinated by the little girl with green eyes and honey-colored braids. She admitted there was no reason they couldn't plant both, and so they did.

The two soon became as inseparable as their homes. They worked together in the garden and played make-believe in nearby Riverside Park. Kit, always the knight, and Greta alternating between being the princess and the dragon. She'd gotten quite good at capturing herself.

When they were older, he built a mechanical dragon, which she armed with an alchemical flamethrower. They only got to use it once. In hindsight, they probably should have warned the local constable before taking it to the park. The trouble had been completely worth it, just to see the look of awestruck glee on Greta's face.

After that, he'd kept the devices he made for her small and limited in destructive potential.

Kit slipped a hand into his pocket, rubbing the smooth polished wooden box which held his latest token of affection. It had taken all his skill, but fortunately only a little money and materials. They were nearly twenty and little had changed between them in fifteen years. While she seemed perfectly content with their friendship, Kit had grown restless and worried. His thoughts turned often to grown up problems and desires, most of which revolved around her.

Inside the box nestled a ring which would hopefully resolve a few of those problems and fulfill his greatest desire. Fashioned with exquisite care after countless hours staring through rows of magnifying glasses, he'd poured his heart into a ring like no other.

Interlocking copper, silver, gold, and steel made an intricate pattern resembling roses and vines. Within its narrow works, the ring held the tiniest music box imaginable. Twisted just so, it would play Greta's favorite tune. A work of master tinkering so sublime, it seemed like magic. The ring displayed his finest work. Determined, he intended to offer it and a proposal of marriage to his best friend.

The lab had grown quiet, the tinkling of glass beakers and jars stilled for a few seconds. Moments when Greta wasn't flitting around like a hummingbird were few and far between. Better act now before he lost his nerve or she set something on fire.

※ ※ ※

Inside the laboratory, Greta frowned in fierce concentration, consumed by the featherfall formulae. The time had come time to add a second solution, and heat it until it turned silvery white. She poured in the vial of lemon-yellow liquid, and the formulae turned bright green. She stirred it, setting it above an oil lamp. She lifted her goggles to her forehead, unable to see through the fog. Now she just had to watch it constantly and remove it from the heat the moment it began to turn white.

She'd barely had a moment to relax when Kit flung the door open, striding into the room. Greta turned in surprise. Her eyes widened at her friend's disheveled appearance.

Kit was always as neat as his perfectly-ordered workshop, his soot-black hair combed as precisely as he tuned the springs in his machines. His overalls and shirt might be smudged with grease, but they'd be starched and pressed beneath the grime, sleeves rolled up past his sinewy forearms.

At this moment, his tan face glistened with sweat. His dark hair stood on end from running both hands through it bracing himself. His wire-rimmed spectacles were pulled off his face and dangled precariously from his breast pocket.

He was wearing his Sunday suit, and it was only Friday.

Greta found this change alarming. Her Kit was as reliable as the sun. Something bad must have happened. Was he on his way to a funeral? Did she know the dearly departed? Her inability to note or remember such social details made Kit her only friend, as well as her oldest and dearest. Well, that along with her tendency to cause violent explosions.

"Good gracious, Kit! Has someone died? Are you feeling ill?" She brushed a lock of amber hair back from her face. She hurried towards him, hand outstretched to check for a fever.

In her distress, she failed to notice the featherfall formulae change to silvery white behind her.

* * *

A concerned motherly reaction was not what Kit had in mind at all. He stepped backward into the doorway, as if that could rewind time so he could begin again.

"No, no, no." He shook his head in frustration. "No one has passed, and I'm perfectly fine." He waved her hand away, trying to brush the irritation from his voice. In his mind, he'd planned this moment with the same detail as one of his mechanical drawings, and it was not going at all according to the plan. Things rarely did where Greta was concerned.

He started again, struggling to find the right words. Improvising had never been his greatest strength.

"Greta." He reached into his pocket for the ring, toying with it nervously. "We're very good friends, aren't we?"

Behind her back, the formulae darkened from silvery white to dull grey.

❋ ❋ ❋

Alarmed at Kit's anxious tone, Greta stepped closer, placing a hand on his shoulder. "Of course! Best friends since we were children." She looked into his warm brown eyes, questions furrowing her brow.

"But we're not children anymore. We've grown up. We have to put childhood behind us. Move into the future." Kit took a deep breath, as if determined to press on while he had her full attention for once. She had utterly forgotten the table of potions behind her.

Greta's quicksilver mind ran a million miles ahead — in the absolute wrong direction.

Kit was leaving. She was certain of it. Three months ago Kit had seen his greatest triumph as a tinker, creating the mechanicals for the main exhibit at the Great Christmas Exposition. The biggest newspapers in the republics had written about his wonderful devices. Now some industrialist must have offered him an engineering position, probably somewhere far away, fulfilling Greta's most dreaded fear.

Kit had come to bid her farewell, leaving childhood and his oldest friend behind.

"Kit, please don't." She turned away, hiding tears. Greta suddenly saw her friend with new eyes, as a grown man. Of course he wanted to move away and seek his fortune. He couldn't stay in his father's house forever, making her clockwork songbirds and cleaning up her catastrophes. She should have expected it, but it still hurt.

As she wiped at the tear sliding down her cheek, the featherfall formulae darkened, its grey liquid swirling ominously like storm clouds.

* ❄ *

Kit was crushed. He'd expected surprise. He'd feared she might ask for time to think about it, or insist they were too young. He had not expected her to reject him outright. He gathered his nerve, determined to convince her. She had no idea how important it was that she marry him, and soon.

As usual, she'd fallen into danger without realizing it.

❄ ❄ ❄

Greta looked up, wiped her eyes and noticed the beaker tittering excitedly over the oil lamp. The featherfall formulae had turned oily black.

Oh dear.

Greta whirled, grabbing Kit's upper arms. She flung her body against his with all her might. Caught off guard, Kit staggered back through the open door. They fell to the ground, Greta landing on top of Kit with a thud. His head smacked against stone pavers, nearly knocking him unconscious.

A resounding "Boom!" from the lab blew the door onto Greta's back, flattening her between heavy oak panels and Kit's chest. The door see-sawed over her back, the upper end hit him in the face and slammed his head against the pavers again. The door did at least protect them as the windows exploded shards of glass.

Thick black smoke poured out the doorless opening and shattered windows. It smelled like scorched maple syrup, with a hint of lemons.

Kit grunted and shoved the door off them. Greta scrambled off him, straightening the wool skirts of her red plaid wrapper. As the smoke cleared, they could see almost every object in the lab was crushed, broken, shattered, or otherwise destroyed. But all the pieces were pressed up against the ceiling. It gave the place the bizarre appearance of a trash heap flipped upside down. Even the broken ends of cracked floorboards seemed to be straining upwards.

The entire shed shuddered. At first, Greta thought it was still shaking from the explosion. Then, with a groan, the shed lurched upwards, its clapboard siding rattling.

Kit regained his feet behind her. He grabbed her around the waist and dragged her backwards. A sudden jerk freed the shed from its foundation, and apparently from the laws of gravity.

It jolted up three feet, tethered for a moment by the water pipe Greta had installed two years before. Another jerk broke that. The shed flew upward like a circus gymnast launched from a trampoline. They watched it disappear into the clouds, narrowly missing a passing airship.

Greta stood agape, staring up at where her laboratory had disappeared. She turned to Kit, as he gazed up at the sky.

"Sweet mercy, Greta. I've always said you'd blow the lab sky high. Never guessed I'd see it happen quite so . . . literally." The absurdity of the situation struck him. He chuckled, then began laughing hysterically, doubled over partly in pain and partly from laughter.

Greta had reached her limit. Kit was going away. She had no proof of her formulae's success. In fact, it had been such a success, all the evidence would soon be in orbit.

She'd lost her lab, and she'd be lucky if Father ever let her near a mortar and pestle again. She looked at Kit in his ruined suit, his broad shoulder visible through a rip in the jacket. A purplish-green lump was forming on his forehead. His crushed spectacles tumbled out of his pocket.

She burst into a sob, turned on her heel and ran through the smoke and spray of water towards her back door. Kit chased her, stammering an apology. It was no good, though. She slammed the door in his face.

* * *

"Greta!" he yelled. "Greta, please, I'm so sorry. Please come back. We need to talk. It's important.

13

I'll help you. . . ." He paused. He had been going to say "clean things up," since that was his usual offer when her experiments took a poor turn. Turning around he could see there was very little mess left that bore removing. The broken pipe spewed a glittering spray of water across the lawn, but most of the debris had ascended with the lab.

It was no use. He could hear her heavy boots stomping up the stairs to her room. Her parents were gone for a week, visiting family and friends in the Republic of Illinois. The last thing either of them needed was the scandal sure to break out if the neighbor ladies, with their predilection for mean-spirited gossip, saw him follow her into the house without a proper chaperone.

Of course, such a scandal might prompt her to accept his proposal, but he was not the sort of man to compromise a lady to get what he wanted. And whether Greta wanted to accept it or not, she was a young lady, not a little girl anymore.

He decided the best course of action was to give her an hour or so to calm down. She'd be out soon enough, trying to figure out how to minimize the damage before her parents came home.

At the thought of her parents, his face flushed with anger. He took a deep breath. Returning home to his workshop would be the best thing right now. Otherwise, he'd be too tempted to tell Greta the troubling things he'd overheard last week. Once they'd both calmed down a bit, he could try again to get her to hear him out. Hopefully, he wouldn't have to warn her what might happen if she didn't.

Through all the uproar and distraction, Kit failed to take much note of a slim, pale man with dark brown, slicked-back hair and facial features sharp enough to etch glass who observed them from the edges of the alley. Even with his dark grey coat and charcoal bowler hat, he seemed to blend a little too well into the background, shimmering in and out of Kit's peripheral vision. As Kit flung open the back door of his own home, the man pulled a black tin raven from within his great coat, whispered to it, and released it before disappearing entirely into the shadows.

CHAPTER 2
DAMAGE CONTROL

Kit stormed through into the kitchen of his parents' home. He yanked off his tie and ruined suit jacket before the door had fully shut behind him. It only took a few minutes before he was cleaned up from the disaster of Greta's laboratory, and dressed in his usual attire. Clad in sturdy work boots, brown breeches, suspenders and a clean shirt with the sleeves rolled up, his first thought was to return to his workshop. Donning a spare pair of spectacles, he began sorting through the neat stacks of metal and gears, in hopes that organizing the parts and materials might help him order his chaotic thoughts.

The workshop was emptier than usual. He'd been doing his level best to sell every device and mechanism as soon as he was finished with it. His stall in the Mechanical Marketplace grew more popular with each passing week. The press he'd received from The Great Christmas Exposition had been a huge blessing. He'd built up a steady stream of regular customers for repair work, and more lucrative commissions were beginning to trickle in as well. It wouldn't be long before he had enough business, and enough savings, to consider moving from the Marketplace stall to a shop of his own.

Which was a very good thing. Greta's freedom was in jeopardy, and he was determined to save her. The loss of the laboratory was going to be the least of their concerns if he couldn't figure out a way around Greta's childish refusal to even listen to his proposal.

She never listened. Especially to something she didn't want to hear. He sighed in exasperation, picking up a wrench and tightening the bolts on a mechanical tea trolley. There were so many things she didn't want to hear these days.

The real world and their impending adulthood was encroaching on Greta's fantasy world with increasing frequency. He'd watched as she fought it with the enthusiasm she'd once applied to fighting their mechanical dragon. He didn't suppose he could blame her. For a man, growing up meant independence and self-determination. For a young woman, it usually meant the exact opposite.

He'd watched with an odd mix of annoyance and amusement as her parents had tried unsuccessfully to make a match for her with eligible young men in the neighborhood. Although they'd tolerated his friendship with their daughter, his status as a tradesman's son placed him a little below their aims for a son-in-law. Greta had never made an issue of the difference in their social stations, but then again, she and her parents rarely saw things the same way. Up until a week ago, he had believed that once his prospects were more established and he had a shop of his own, he could sway them to his cause.

Annoyance had turned to outrage just a week ago, when he'd overheard her father grousing about the cost of supporting her. Greta's father always assiduously avoided mentioning her alchemical antics in polite company. Evidently, he found the cost of raising a daughter was a more fitting subject for conversation.

Unaware of Kit's presence nearby, Jonah Singleton had told his companion he was considering advertising his troublesome child as a mail-order bride in the territories. Having exhausted the heirs of old money in Missouri Republic, he now found himself weighing the merits of *nouveau riche* gold miners and speculators out West.

It had taken every ounce of Kit's self-control not to run out from behind his Marketplace stall and beat the man to a bloody pulp. Instead, he'd crushed the small clockwork device he'd been holding into a wadded ball of copper and tin. The idea of Greta being shipped off as some stranger's wife had felt like a shard of ice stabbing his heart. A bitter cold chill had settled on him as he realized Singleton seemed to be really considering it in earnest.

Although he'd loved her since the day they met, he'd intended to wait until he'd managed to open a tinker shop of his own before asking for Greta's hand. That day in the marketplace, he'd grimly realized what he had would have to be enough. He had found a small shop in the Craftsman's Quarter with a few rooms above it which they could afford, assuming the commissions and repair work continued to pour in.

He just hoped Singleton hadn't already firmly decided to sell her out West. He hoped the man would count his daughter's happiness worth something. Hoped, but feared otherwise. As Kit got older, he stopped expecting people to be guided by kindness, especially when greed pointed to a different course of action.

Greta still had a childlike trust in others' good intentions. Kit was keenly aware of how the world worked, and the casual cruelty around him. He observed others with the same quiet intensity he devoted to tinkering. Most people took an instant dislike to anyone different.

The world didn't make room for people like Greta, who didn't fit the typical mold. She was like one of his devices; clever, unique and beautiful. If he didn't step in, society would keep squeezing Greta in its relentless grip until she conformed into a bland, boring factory-made doll. It was a tragedy he was determined to prevent.

The bolt he'd been tightening broke off in his hands as he remembered how angry he'd been that day. Sighing with exasperation, he looked around the workshop for some other task. There was the box of clockwork angels, left over from the Exposition. He and Greta had been working together, attempting to find a more practical use for them. The ornate carving work on the pieces had been particularly well done, but few people had use for decorations which flew around singing Christmas carols during the rest of the year.

Greta had suggested they might make a reasonably good burglar alarm. They'd look like perfectly harmless lawn ornaments, but with the proper punch card, they could react to unexpected movement. Even if all they did was make a huge racket and beat upon the intruder with their harps, they could probably prevent many robberies.

Unfortunately, he was just too distracted to trust himself working on such delicate mechanisms. Unless he wanted a workshop full of more broken devices, he'd be better off taking a walk to calm his nerves. He set the angel aside, grabbed his coat and hat, and headed off to the park.

* * *

When life's exasperations exceeded his considerable patience, Kit found a brisk walk at Riverside Park usually restored his equilibrium. The bright March sun didn't quite banish the chill in the air, but the exertion of walking soon warmed him up.

He could see the shining towers of the

downtown business district above the trees. The St. Louis Municipal Monorail zipped through the sky along on its sleek silvery track. Airships soared by, dropping to clear customs after arriving from the Republic of Illinois. A border ferry chugged across the Mississippi River dividing the two nations.

He trudged past an old woman sitting on a bench before turning onto a less-frequented footpath, anxious to be away from other people.

He wondered what the Singletons' reaction would be when they returned from Illinois to discover the shed missing. If they were delayed at least a little while at the border, it would give Greta a brief reprieve, but that seemed unlikely. It was not as though they were in the habit of carrying back contraband from a visit to Greta's elderly maiden aunt in Peoria.

Although things had been fairly peaceful among the Republics for the past decade, the papers still hinted at simmering unrest and secret alliances. Still, Illinois and Missouri had a long history of friendly relations, so the border passing was just a formality.

Politics was another grown-up concern which tugged at the edges of his mind while seeming to leave Greta entirely untouched. His father fought in one of the continental wars. Kit knew from his father's stories how quickly a seemingly trivial disagreement between nations could escalate into violence.

Forty-eight independent countries comprised the North American continent now, with more territories gaining immigrants in the hopes of reaching the population required for independent nation status every day. Some had rich resources, while others struggled. He supposed human nature dictated those with little should envy the rich, and those with plenty should guard it jealously.

He'd scoffed when a friend suggested the continent, with its intricate alliances and rivalries, could be one violent moment away from plunging into a World War. Still, he supposed stranger things had happened. He had, after all, just watched an entire garden shed laboratory ascend to the heavens.

He couldn't help chuckling as he walked through the sun-dappled park, remembering the look of mingled excitement and dismay on Greta's face as the lab had taken flight. Despite the trouble it was sure to cause, he couldn't deny it was a moment of sheer wonder.

His head still throbbed, and he might need to see a doctor about his shoulder, but one thing was certain. Life with Greta would never be boring or predictable. She'd created a concoction which could defy gravity. Failures and explosions aside, he believed she could accomplish anything she set her mind to do. And he was determined to make sure she didn't lose the freedom to pursue her dreams.

Becoming the young lady of quality her parents wanted would mean she'd have to give up everything that made her happy — most likely including Kit. While his parents were delighted he'd found a trade so young, her dabbling in alchemy was a source of constant consternation to her family. They expected her to be absorbed in the rules of etiquette and pay meticulous attention appearances. Instead, she was fascinated with bending the laws of science and couldn't possibly care less how she looked or what others thought of her.

When obsessed with an idea for a new alchemical formulae, she'd neither see nor hear anything else, like a cab horse wearing blinders. Her failure to acknowledge his romantic gestures like the clockwork canary were exasperating, but hardly surprising.

Oh, she'd squealed with delight when he'd given it to her, and wrapped him in a tight but all-too-brief embrace. But the knowing look, the understanding that it was a gift from a young man to the woman he admired, never came. He was just her Kit, the same Kit she'd grubbed in the garden with as a child, the same Kit who'd rubbed warmth back into her hands while calling her a silly goose when she'd nearly frozen herself.

He was such a constant presence in her life, she couldn't see even him. At least, not as a suitor.

He had to concede that, given the treatment she usually gave suitors, that might be a point in his favor. He was fairly sure she'd coated the last one's hat and jacket with an itching formulae, judging by how ferociously he'd been scratching as he stormed off. Kit's workshop was an excellent vantage point to see the results of one gentlemen after another having a very unsatisfactory visit with his neighbors.

Midday sun poured through the pale green leaves and buds, hinting at the hope of a spring that still felt far away. He pulled off his coat and hung it over his other arm as a breeze ruffled his hair. He still intended to finish that proposal, and it would be best if he weren't soaked with sweat when he did. The path turned, meandering through a thick patch of cedar and pine. Their dark, muted green broke up the monotonous greys and browns of the landscape, which hadn't yet shifted from winter's palette to spring's.

He frowned, wondering if he'd misinterpreted Greta's response to his romantic gestures. Maybe she'd been ignoring his intentions on purpose. What if she really didn't return his affections? He'd always believed she loved him, but what if she truly felt only friendship?

While he didn't doubt she'd do whatever she thought was the kindest thing in such a situation, predicting exactly what Greta's mind would consider "the kindest thing" was a puzzle that didn't bear thinking about. She'd once decided the best way to help him get rid of a cold was to give him an alchemical tisane designed to make him sneeze continuously.

"It'll clear your system faster!" she'd insisted. He'd declined her concoction, but the neighbor's cat must have licked up a bit of it after they'd poured it out. The poor creature never did nose around the laboratory after it finally recovered.

Her odd reaction to his proposal attempt puzzled him, and admittedly wounded his pride. More importantly, it made him afraid for her. Being certain she wasn't rejecting him for another man was cold comfort. Especially when her parents were so determined to marry her off.

The Singletons had inherited legacies from both sides of the family. Margaret Singleton was unfailingly sweet, if a bit exasperated. Jonah was something of a bear, though. Kit could never understand why he showed such little affection for his only daughter. Kit had no doubt the man would sell her to the highest bidder and consider himself lucky to be rid of her.

※ ※ ※

She was beautiful, but she was so much more than that. He wanted her love, but he also wanted to protect her ability to be her own person. He couldn't imagine anyone else loving her as much as he did. He certainly didn't believe another man would bother getting to know her as well as he did. They were generally focused on her more visible assets, although Greta seemed oblivious to the attention.

She didn't even notice the leering looks she received from men during their daily walks in the park. Just earlier this week, a fair-haired young man in a black suit had followed her home from the herbalist's. Kit had caught him poking around her laboratory after her parents left. He'd run the man off, but when he'd asked Greta about the man, she'd said he had only been asking about her alchemical experiments. She'd nearly forgotten the conversation had even happened by the time he'd asked her about it.

"What else could he have possibly wanted with me, Kit?" she'd asked, laughing.

He'd been tempted to pull her into his arms and show her exactly what any sane man would want with her. Instead, he'd just shook his head and told her to show a little caution where strange men were concerned. Her own imagination always held her attention far more than what went on around her.

Now here he was, finding himself distractedly imagining kissing her, when he needed to be devising a plan to get her married to him. Or, if she was absolutely opposed to being his wife, figuring out some other way to avoid her father's scheme. He could hardly imagine a person less well-suited to life in the wild and uncivilized frontier than Greta.

The park trail sloped upwards, and he was beginning to feel warm and settled again as he smiled, thinking about her two obsessions: music and alchemy. She couldn't sing or play a note, but she adored music. She appreciated beauty, although she wore simple, frugal clothing, preferring to spend whatever money she had on gramophone cylinders or alchemy supplies. Her practical attire had earned her the derision of the more fashionable young ladies in the neighborhood.

Her disregard for others' opinions meant the mean-spirited barbs rarely hurt her. Unfortunately, it also meant she rarely listened to advice. What would she do without him if he couldn't convince her to accept his proposal? Her spontaneity and curiosity often got her into the most appalling situations.

He'd happily keep rescuing her from these misadventures if he could. Greta viewed the world with the innocent optimism of an alchemist, seeing only possibilities. He viewed it with an engineer's eye for detail, seeing every broken cog and twisted spring of human frailty. He realized, even if Greta didn't, what a damaged, dangerous place it was. Eventually, her naive innocence would attract human predators. Whether she loved him or not, he wouldn't let her fall into their hands.

He'd arrived at the footbridge over a stream flowing into the river. One of the more peaceful spots in the park, from here you could hardly tell you were in one of the great cities of the continent, the Gateway to the West. He felt the last of his anger dissipate, as if it dropped into the stream to be swept away to the mighty Mississippi.

He could never stay upset with Greta for long. She had probably settled down as well. He should head back and help her set things right, at least as much as they could. There wasn't time to rebuild the shed, and he could hardly spare the money for materials right now, but perhaps they could figure something out together. Perhaps he could get her to listen to his proposal, too.

The sound of steam engines and pumping hydraulics caught his attention. Mechanical automatons called 'gens, from the English word "engine" and the French word for people, must be nearby. They sounded like miniature railway trains, or the snorting of a wild beast.

He puzzled over the sound. It could be a household servant, but he'd never seen several outdoors together in the city. Even the wealthy usually had only one, and kept them home where they wouldn't get damaged. Cheaper agricultural 'gens went out to the fields in groups, but he was miles from the nearest farm.

His curiosity was soon answered. The clanking metal and snorting engine announced a mechanical wolf. Steam and smoke puffed out of its nostrils. Red optical lenses glowed within a copper canine skull. Sharp, perfectly shaped steel teeth ringed its open mouth. Four identical beasts stalked out of the wood after it. With a purpose that seemed eerily lifelike, the pack of metal wolves advanced on the footbridge.

CHAPTER 3
CLEANING UP HER MESS

After she'd had a good cry, Greta brushed the dirt and debris from her hair, washed her face and hands, and changed from her ruined plaid wrapper into a green poplin dress. Her amber braids were still wrapped around her head. Loose hair could fall into formulae or fire; she enjoyed neither. After donning a fresh pinafore, gloves and a knit hat, she headed back to the garden to address the scene of her latest failure.

She grabbed a wrench from the toolbox in the pantry. Her first mission was closing off the water line spraying a fountain over the remains of her laboratory.

Early March was still bitter cold, and now she was wet. Father would be outraged when he discovered she'd lost the garden shed, just as he'd predicted. Well, maybe not exactly as he'd predicted. After all, she hadn't actually destroyed the lab. There was no way of knowing where it was, but the last she'd seen of it, the small building had still been more or less intact. Father would probably not appreciate the difference. Still, the more she cleaned up before he and Mother returned, the less severe her punishment would be.

Neighbors glared from their windows as usual. They used to come out and complain. After one matron had gotten violently ill from the fumes of a previous experiment, they tended to rant from the safety of their homes. She was lucky no one had run for the constable yet.

Even if she managed to convince Father the accident wasn't her fault, the respectable ladies of the neighborhood would take this as yet another opportunity to pull Mother aside and insist she find a husband to "put that girl in her place." According to everyone but Kit, her place was sitting in some parlor keeping her opinions to herself and letting her talents go to waste.

Where was Kit, anyway? She wanted to apologize for how they'd parted, and she'd probably need his help getting the water shut off.

When the laboratory had broken free, it had twisted and bent some of the copper pipes. The shut-off valve appeared to be hopelessly jammed open. She struggled with the wrench, trying to coax the valve closed and stop the spraying water.

"Excuse me, Miss. You seem like you could use a little help?"

Greta dropped the wrench in surprise and spun around. A tall, broad-shouldered young man in a black suit stood in the alley. His scarlet four-in-hand tie, and the red rose in his lapel, stood out sharply against the black wool of his suit. Blond hair stuck out from under his hat and a friendly smile was almost hidden beneath a tawny beard. He looked familiar, but she couldn't quite place him.

"Have we met?" She picked up the wrench and resolved to keep a good solid grip on it. Hadn't Kit just reminded her last week not to be too trusting of strangers?

"Briefly. I believe we may have spoken at Thompson's Herbalist Market. You're an alchemist, aren't you? You were there to pick up some ingredients." He smiled pleasantly, as if they were discussing the weather at a tea party.

"That's right! I remember you. You seemed very interested in the items in my basket." She frowned at him suspiciously, trying to remember what formulae she'd been working on that particular occasion. Was it the one she'd concocted to give constables the tracking abilities of bloodhounds? He must not be from this part of town. Most of her neighbors hurried the other direction when they saw her carrying parcels, as opposed to approaching for a closer look.

"You don't see a young lady carrying those particular ingredients very often. I'm sorry — I've interrupted you in the middle of some important repairs, obviously. I only noticed the. . . ." He waved a hand in the direction of the spouting water.

"Catastrophe? Disaster?"

"I was going to say 'water.' Or possibly 'accident.' I realize this is the second time I've been so forward as to speak without a proper introduction in as many weeks. But I can assure you, I only want to help. You seemed to be having some trouble with that valve."

Greta frowned. "I'm terribly sorry. Yes, please, I'd be most grateful if you could lend a hand. I would love to tell you I'm not usually this rude, but unfortunately, the truth is I'm rarely this polite. I was hoping a friend of mine might return and help, but it seems he's busy elsewhere at the moment." She frowned at the alley, but there was no sign of Kit, so she reluctantly handed the young man the wrench.

He sidled around the spray, and managed to close off the valve in less than a minute, without even getting his lovely black suit damp.

"Well, you're quite a competent fellow, aren't you? What did you say your name was again?"

"Simms. Cornelius Simms. However, my friends call me Neal. And you are?"

"Greta Jane Singleton." She stuck out her hand; since he was still holding the wrench, he had to shift it awkwardly to his other hand to shake hers.

"Well, Greta, it seems as if your formulae didn't work out quite as you'd planned?"

She couldn't help but laugh. "No, it actually worked far better than I could have ever anticipated. I just wasn't prepared for the unmitigated success of that particular experiment."

He gave her a puzzled look. "What were you attempting, when success left a rather obvious hole in your property and what appears to be a missing outbuilding?" He gestured at the soaked and empty shed foundation.

"You wouldn't believe me if I told you."

She caught the ghost of a frown passing his face. "Nothing improper, I hope?"

The Alchemists Guild had strict regulations. Greta's parents hadn't even let her take the examination to be registered as an apothecary, much less a full alchemist. There were many formulae she couldn't legally attempt. Of course, this young man didn't know she wasn't registered.

"Oh, no. Nothing prohibited by the Guild. I had an idea to create a formulae which could . . . well . . . achieve an unprecedented, but completely legal effect."

Experiments attempting to create entirely new formulae were something of a loophole in the Guild's restrictions. Aside from formulae intended to create or harm living things, if no one had successfully created a particular formulae or effect, anyone was welcome to try it, presuming they didn't use outlawed substances. Of course, any unintended injury, death or property damage was subject to the same laws as any other activity.

Mr. Simms looked at the empty space where the lab had once been, and raised his eyebrows in an unspoken question.

She sighed. It's wasn't as if it hadn't happened in full view of the nosy neighbors. If he was really that curious, he could ask and would certainly hear the story from any number of witnesses. Most likely with some colorful embellishments.

"I was trying to create an atmospheric buoyancy formulae. I got distracted at a critical moment."

Simms eyes grew wide in surprise.

"Then you mean . . . the outbuilding? The whole thing?"

"Sprang skyward and flew away like an untethered airship." She nodded solemnly and waved in the direction it had disappeared.

The young man's jaw dropped in amazement. For a moment, she found herself reconsidering the wisdom of her candor. The vague but appalling rumors about how the Guild responded to renegades ensured her discretion most of the time. While she had done nothing technically forbidden, she had no desire to tempt fate. Since the incident with the clockwork dragon, she'd followed the letter of the law, if not the spirit.

She'd managed to obtain some very rare ingredients, but she scrupulously avoided the illegal ones. But the neighbors didn't care. They still regarded her as a public nuisance. Their poor opinion of her didn't stop them from tapping on her door when they needed a healing salve or prevent a few from hinting if she ever just happened to stumble upon a love potion, they'd take the illegal concoction off her hands.

Now a total stranger knew she'd skirted the very edges of the law. She worried the young man would feel obliged to contact the authorities. Her father's property had been damaged and Kit had been injured, even though he'd never report it.

"Mr. Simms, I can assure you, my experiments rarely turn out this badly. And none of my materials were prohibited for use by someone of my status." She didn't specifically say her status was unregistered, hoping he would assume she meant she was a licensed journeyman alchemist, or at least an apothecary.

Simms nodded amiably at her, seeming unconcerned about the propriety of her experiment after he'd gotten over the sheer novelty of it.

"Well, I'm sorry it didn't work out as you'd hoped, Miss Singleton. Or perhaps congratulations on your unprecedented success?" He chuckled a bit and she couldn't help but laugh as well. "Actually, I must apologize once again. You see, it was no accident that I happened upon you, at Thompson's or today. I was sent here by the Alchemists Guild to see if you might be a good candidate for membership."

Greta's eyes nearly bugged out of their sockets. The Alchemists Guild had noticed her? She wasn't sure whether to be delighted or terrified.

"You're an alchemist? With the Guild?" Her voice squeaked a little as she tried to gather her wits.

"No, not precisely. I work with the Boyle Society. We're . . . well, consider us something of an adjunct to the Alchemists Guild. It's very difficult to get actual alchemists to leave their laboratories, so we handle some of the more strenuous activities for them."

Greta laughed nervously. The bit about getting alchemists out of the lab was undoubtedly true. But the nature of the "strenuous" activity the Boyle Society engaged in was a cause for some concern.

"So, you've been sent here to report on me? What are you going to tell them, if I may ask?" She brushed her suddenly sweaty hands on her pinafore.

"Considering the unprecedented success of your atmospheric buoyancy formulae, I think it would be best for everyone if you continued your studies under the supervision of the Guild." He broke into a wide grin, setting her at ease.

"Then you're not reporting me as a renegade?" The relief in her voice was palpable.

"Of course not, Miss Singleton. Anyone who spent more than a few minutes around you could tell there's nothing maleficent about you. Not to mention, your gift for subterfuge and subtlety, two key ingredients in any villain, seems. . . ." He looked up at the ruins of the laboratory, "Decidedly lacking."

He pulled a pocket watch out and frowned at her. "I'm afraid I must be going. Will your friend be along soon to help?"

"I'm sure he will. Thank you for your assistance, Mr. Simms."

"In that case, I'd ask you to take my card. I need to file a report with the Guild, before we can move forward. If you have any concerns in the meantime, you can wire me."

As the young man sauntered off down the alley towards the next street, she began to wonder where Kit could be. At some point, she would need to apologize for how she'd behaved and let him tell her his news. Now at least, she had a little good news of her own to share.

If the Alchemists Guild recruited her directly, surely her parents would see reason and allow her to continue studying. It couldn't completely take the sting out of the idea of Kit leaving, but it at least made it a little easier for her to put a good face on it. She was determined to try to be happy for him. Perhaps the situation wasn't as dire as she'd thought, and he would be able to visit her often.

Whatever opportunity he'd been offered, he deserved it. He'd been working so hard at his devices for years. He deserved all the recognition the world could offer. Sometimes, it just didn't seem fair. She'd worked as hard as he had, and exhibited just as much talent in her chosen field, but up until today, any recognition she'd achieved had been more like infamy.

She leaned down and plucked a shiny bit of metal, half buried in debris. It was the little clockwork canary. It must have been blown out the window. The delicate machinery which gave it song was probably destroyed, but the brass bird was still a beautiful piece of work.

Why did Kit's efforts turn out so beautifully, while hers resulted in property damage and outraged bystanders? She blamed the nature of their different passions, which matched their temperaments. Mechanical work suited his precise, methodical nature. It was predictable, a simple matter of cause and effect, even if he did often surprise her with what he could coax out of cogs, gears, engines and springs. Kit's devices might fail to work, or run out of control, but he always included a failsafe.

There was no failsafe in alchemy. Alchemy aimed to create powerful reactions beyond all calculation. It involved transforming elemental substances into new materials with amazing, unexpected properties. Of course, their friendship mirrored the Great Partnership, which had resulted in combining machinery with alchemy to create the modern conveniences society enjoyed.

Over a century ago, alchemists ceased chasing the philosopher's stone, a material that supposedly could turn base metal to gold and grant eternal life and youth. Instead, they applied their prodigious minds to more practical possibilities. Working alongside the great engineering minds of the Age of Reason, they had created alchemically-treated coal which could power an agricultural automaton for weeks. The invention of 'gens had ended slavery in the Republics just as they'd won freedom from the European monarchies. The Great Partnership made many of the current technological marvels possible.

Like the Great Partnership, she and Kit worked on several projects together, combining their abilities to create devices neither could have managed alone. Some of her favorite memories were of the two of them working alongside each other.

Still, there were strict limits to mixing alchemy and machinery, and with good reason. Greta had heard horror stories of renegade alchemists trying to create artificial life with homunculi or, worse, by reanimating dead creatures. She recoiled at the idea of someone trying to build a creature who could think, but couldn't feel; who couldn't die, but wasn't really alive.

But renegade deviants were the exception. Most alchemists were like Greta, interested in exploring new and wonderful possibilities for mankind. Greta loved alchemy for the same reason Kit loved tinkering: it matched her spontaneous, unpredictable nature. At moments like this, she felt just a bit more predictability might have been desirable.

At least most of the debris had joined the laboratory. After she swept up the broken glass, she only had to contend with the fallen door. She should probably move it out of the alley. Peddlers' carts chugged and rattled through the alley all the time, selling wares to housekeepers who found it convenient to step out the back door for a few trinkets, some soap and a bit of gossip.

She lifted the door, shoving it into the depression formed by the laboratory's foundation. Looking down for more glass, she spotted a small wooden box pressed into the soft earth where the door had been.

Kit must have dropped it.

She dug it up, dusting off the dirt. Polished cedar, it looked like something Kit might have made. He preferred metal, but was also skilled at woodworking.

Greta considered it for a moment, consumed with curiosity. She and Kit did not keep secrets from one another. She should just make sure her explosion hadn't damaged or destroyed whatever he'd put in it.

Kit had lined it with red velvet, her favorite color. A gorgeous clockwork ring sat undamaged inside. She found it breathtakingly beautiful, his best work yet. The roses reminded her of their first meeting, and the time they'd spent tending the garden. She held it up to the light. The engraving inside read "G - Yours for eternity. - K."

Greta dropped the ring and box in shock.

She fell to her knees, scrambling to find them. As she put the ring back in the box, the pieces clicked into place.

Kit wasn't leaving. He hadn't come to say goodbye. The disheveled hair, his nervousness, the glasses tucked into his pocket, the talk of being grown up, all made sense now. Kit wanted to marry her.

Kit wanted to marry *her*? What on earth was he thinking? She'd nearly killed both of them. If Kit wanted a wife, he'd picked an awful prospect.

She needed to find him and talk some sense into him. He was handsome and smart and absolutely wonderful. Surely he could have almost any woman in the republic, certainly any young lady in St. Louis. Not his misfit friend, a creature unfit for matrimony. Even the most powerful alchemy couldn't transform her into a demure, domestic young lady. She couldn't allow Kit to bind himself to a walking disaster.

She tucked the box into her apron pocket, put on a heavy cloak, and headed for Riverside Park as fast as her high-button shoes could carry her. He always went there when he was upset. She wanted to catch him before he returned. The park offered more privacy than the alley, with neighborhood gossips peering out their windows.

CHAPTER 4
ON THE RUN

Kit stood as still as possible on the footbridge, staring at the steam-powered creatures stalking towards him. Despite the fear bubbling up in his chest, he couldn't help being fascinated by the wolves with their natural, purposeful movement. The most advanced 'gens he'd heard of could stiffly follow simple instructions. These mimicked the behavior of natural wolves. The craftsmanship was superb, although it was a little hard to fully appreciate it while feeling like a main course presented on a platter.

No Lovelace engine could produce this kind of animation. After their adventure with the mechanical dragon, Greta had told him alchemy could simulate a kind of artificial life. But attempting to create such a construct was strictly forbidden throughout the civilized world. She refused to tell him even the theory of how it could be accomplished, a good sign it was too foul a practice to even bear talking about.

Who would create a pack of unliving predators and set them loose in a public park?

He backed slowly over the bridge. The ominous sound of more mechanical beasts approached behind him. Four more smoking, clanking metal wolves slunk towards him, their red eyes fixed and fathomless.

Steam huffed out their open maws, the vapor condensing into drips like saliva running down polished steel teeth. Spiked scales of brass and steel ringed each creature's neck like a ruff of grey and gold fur. Eerie red light glowed from glass optics, and a shimmer of alchemical enchantment traced the outline of every beast.

Unarmed and alone, running was his only chance.

Kit leapt over the bridge railing, splashing to a jarring landing in the shallow gravel-covered creek bed. He bolted downstream, his boots sloshing through the shallow water and mud.

The wolves pursued in a heartbeat. Their screeching, grinding gears and joints imitated howls. The snorting of their engines closed in on him.

He yelled, hoping someone would hear him and come to help, but he'd seen no one but an old woman on his way to the footbridge. At midday the park was crowded with people, but in late afternoon it was nearly deserted. He scanned the trees and rocks, looking for a place to hide. There appeared to be no refuge in sight. The wolves were too close on his heels. In the time it would take him to try climbing even the nearest tree branch, they'd be on top of him.

And he was about to run out of ground.

He could smell the river nearby. Just ahead, the creek bed dropped precipitously over a cliff where it emptied into the Mississippi. Once there, maybe he could scramble down and find handholds in the trees and bushes, working his way to a populated area. The wolves were magnificent pieces of machinery, but even real wolves would struggle to scale the steep angle of the muddy river bank. Their heavy metal bodies would tumble straight into the water in the attempt.

He flung his coat away, hoping to distract them. Sliding over the embankment, he grabbed a handful of exposed roots, digging his shoes into the soft mud. None of the wolves followed him over the edge.

He sighed in relief, then the roots tore free and the mud crumbled beneath him. He scrambled, clawing at the side of the cliff, praying to find something strong enough to hold him. Clods of dirt tumbled into his face, causing him to cough, spit and blink. He slid inexorably towards the churning brown water. Kit had learned to swim as a boy, but even strong swimmers were often lost to the terrible currents of the mighty Mississippi.

Nearly halfway down, he managed to grab something that didn't slip away from his grasp. His fingers closed around an outstretched branch. He gripped it for dear life with one hand, then swung around to grab it with the other. He tried to brace his legs against the bank, but it was just too steep and slippery. The dirt crumbled under his shoes. As his body swayed, the branch creaked in complaint.

He'd been right. The wolves wouldn't follow him over the cliff. Apparently, they were smarter than he was.

Now what?

He looked down, hoping to spot a passing riverboat. Even a leaky rowboat would have been a welcome sight. Nothing bobbed in the water nearby except a few bleached driftwood logs and two curious Mallard ducks.

As he dangled above the river, his arms aching, a small airship moved rounded the bend towards him. Built for speed, its small gondola would hold only a pilot and a few passengers. He screamed at the dirigible.

"Hey! Ho, there! I need help! Hey!"

They must have heard or seen him. The airship glided alongside him, although not nearly fast enough to suit Kit. Its slow, languorous movement seemed designed to test his nerves.

The branch bent and groaned beneath his weight. At long last, the airship slowed to a stop a few yards away. The name "Aeolus" was painted on the whitewashed wood in fine gilt script. The balloon was sky-blue silk.

The carriage door sprung open, and a pilot dressed in deep blue velvet livery reached through the opening. The man held a harpoon gun. For a moment, Kit feared he intended to shoot him with it. Being harpooned by a complete stranger would certainly be no stranger than being chased by a slavering pack of steam-powered predators. The laws of probability seemed to have taken the day off.

"Be still, boy! Unless you'd like to get skewered." Kit stilled and held his breath, closing his eyes.

The harpoon whizzed past him, embedding itself deep into the dirt wall of the cliff. A white rope extended inches away, tethered to the airship.

"Come aboard, boy!" the pilot shouted. "That branch cannot hold long!" A series of cracking pops from the branch confirmed the truth of that statement.

Kit sucked in a deep breath and lunged for the rope. He let go of the branch with his other hand just as it broke in half. How long the harpoon could stay stuck in the dirt was the next problem, but he intended to be safely aboard the airship before he discovered the answer. His arms burned with exertion, and he was grateful he'd only had a light breakfast.

Doing mechanical work might have lowered his status in society, but it was currently saving his skin. If not for the strength he'd built up wielding a wrench and bending metal, he'd have surely fallen to his death.

Hand over hand, he worked his way to the door. When he reached it, the pilot grabbed him by his suspenders and dragged him aboard. Kit rested a moment on his hands and knees, shaking from exertion. The gondola swayed gently beneath him, but it was far more stable than the branch or the rope had been. He'd always wanted to ride in an airship, but right at that moment, all he wanted was to feel his feet on solid ground again.

Once he caught his breath, he realized the gondola was occupied. A skirt of icy blue satin brushed the polished wooden planks of the deck near his face. A cold breeze blew across the open gondola, causing him to shiver.

He looked up to see a stunning woman with luminous pale skin. Her platinum hair was coiled into a tight, fashionable chignon, topped by a tiny sapphire-colored hat whose miniscule veil seemed flecked with diamonds.

A pale blue satin underskirt lay under a velvet bustled gown of the same deep blue as her hat. The lady's shoulders were covered with a white fur cape, and she wore long white gloves. Eyes the same pale blue as the satin gazed at him through a pair of opera glasses. She slowly lowered them, giving him a look of cool appraisal.

She ran one hand across the lush velvet bench where she sat. The pilot returned to the enclosed wheelhouse at the bow of the airship.

The propellers at the stern whirred to life, and the ship angled away from the cliff. As they slowly rose, Kit could see the ledge where the wolves had been. They were gone now, disappeared as swiftly and mysteriously as they'd arrived. His coat lay on the ground, ripped to pieces.

He couldn't remember the last time he'd destroyed two coats in one day.

It might be difficult to convince anyone but Greta he'd really encountered such strange and dangerous creatures. Should they report it to the Alchemists Guild immediately, or try to puzzle out the mystery on their own?

Greta would probably want to report it to the authorities, but some part of him relished the challenge of figuring it out. If there was a reward, it might be the nest egg he needed to secure their future.

He'd think about that once he was safely home. In the meantime, he needed to thank his mysterious benefactress. He managed to rise up to a kneeling position, although he was still too lightheaded from the ordeal to risk standing. He looked at the woman, who sneered at him as if he were a mud-coated puppy who'd just run across her priceless oriental rug. His face turned red in embarrassment. Best to give thanks and apologies, and get off her expensive airship before he did any more damage.

"I can't thank you enough, Ma'am," he said, still a little breathless. "I'm forever in your debt."

"Yes, you are, my dear." The frosty tones of the woman's voice matched the chill wind brushing his cheeks. "Not coincidentally, it's a debt you may spend forever repaying."

Kit gave her a confused look. She lifted a gloved hand as if preparing to blow him a kiss. A powder which sparkled like snow flew from her palm into his face. Kit felt all emotion, even his great surprise, fade into nothing.

CHAPTER 5
THE CASE OF THE MISSING MECHANIC

Greta arrived at the park, but Kit was nowhere to be found. She soon discovered a small crowd had gathered around the bridge spanning the little creek.

The constable waved a baton overhead, shouting for order. She was pleased to see his mustache, beard and eyebrows had mostly grown back after the encounter with their mechanical dragon. Perhaps he'd forgotten all about it.

"What's happened?" Greta asked a boy standing at the edge of the glade. Over his head, she spotted the constable glaring at her.

Hasn't forgotten the dragon then. Oh, well.

"Some fool's leapt to his death!" the boy cried. "Some folk saw him through the brush, runnin' toward the river, and he ain't come back."

Greta felt a cold hand reach into her chest, giving her heart a painful squeeze.

"The constable thinks the feller lost his sweetheart. Some folks are sayin' wolves chased him, but that's hogwash. My pa says there ain't been wolves in the city in years."

The constable seemed exasperated. Several people were shouting questions at him, which he ignored. He was leaning down, intent in conversation with an old woman who was gesturing wildly.

Taking advantage of his distraction, Greta slipped to the creek bed. It looked like someone had jumped from the bridge and run downstream. Was it Kit? Looking at the footprints, it could have been. Greta examined the soft mud near the edge of the creek and saw pawprints. But they were much deeper than they should have been, as if the animal had been heavier than even a great hound. The tracks all led down the stream bed and along its banks, towards the low trees and brambles hanging over the river.

The more she saw of the pawprints, the more scared she felt. There were so many of them, at least a half dozen. Each print was perfectly formed, as if pressed into the earth with a metal seal. Kit's tracks were all but lost among them.

She spotted something dark in the brush out of the corner of her eye, and bolted towards it, her breath held.

Please be all right.

Kit's jacket was torn to pieces.

Greta screamed, falling to her knees. The people nearby rushed towards her as she howled in anguish. Someone had clearly slid over the edge of the cliff. A freshly-snapped tree branch was the only thing between the cliff and the churning water of the Mississippi.

No kind brown eyes looked up at her. No voice called out from another ledge or handhold. A steamboat glided across the water a half mile away, careless of the fact that the world had stopped spinning.

Gone.

Dear God, no. He can't be gone! Not when . . . Not after. . . .

Greta sobbed, her face buried in her muddy skirt. Murmuring voices surrounded her, and hands grasped her arms, pulling her away from the cliff.

"Must be the girl."

"Think she spurned him, and he jumped?"

"Well, keep a good grip on her. Can't have her following him over."

"There, there, chile. You just come along with me, honey. It'll be all right, girl."

The old woman who'd been talking with the constable tugged her gently but insistently towards a nearby hill. She settled Greta on the grass and turned to the gawkers.

"You all go on now. You're scarin the poor chile to death. Can't you see she's had a awful shock? I'll take care of her. Just find that poor boy."

The constable whispered to the woman, glowering at Greta, and turned back to look over the river's edge. The mass of people moved towards the cliff, hoping to be the first to spot the body.

"You all right, honey?" the old woman asked.

"You back in yer right mind?"

Greta nodded weakly. She was as right-minded as she'd ever been, which wasn't saying much.

"Then don't make a peep. I'm gonna tell you somethin. Don't be screamin and gettin everybody's attention." The woman moved her head close to Greta's, as if looking for signs of injury, and whispered in her ear "Yer young man did not die in the river."

Greta grabbed the woman's arms so hard she yelped in pain. "What did you see?"

"There was wolves after that boy. If the good Lord lets me live to a hundred, I hope I never see the like again. Metal wolves, breathin smoke like the hounds of Hell." The old woman pressed a hand against her chest, glancing over her shoulder at the constable, who was doing his best to disperse the curious mob.

"The boy went over the edge, but he didn't fall. I seen it from these trees. He hung on to them scrub cedars. I turned to run for help and saw a balloon come round. Came up quick as a wink, just like they was waitin, and pulled your boy aboard. I heard a loud whistle, and them wolves ran off."

"But why?"

"Why didn't they just set him down after the wolves left?" The woman glanced nervously over her shoulder again. The constable was out of earshot. "They wasn't rescuin that boy. They was capturin him. Those wolves run him to ground just like huntin dogs. Whoever took him on board that ship, they're up to no good. I'd stake my life on it."

"How could you possibly know that?"

"For one thing, the ship was painted white and blue. My old eyes are still pretty sharp, but I had trouble spotting 'em. You know what a bad mess it is when them airships collide. Wouldn't nobody make theirs hard to see on purpose, unless they had a reason to avoid bein seen. And I'll tell ya another thing — they're mixed up with some of them alchemists, and I don't trust nobody who meddles with that nonsense."

Greta frowned. "What makes you think they're involved with alchemy?"

"When I seen the wolves, I ran for help. Stumbled onto some greasy dark-haired feller in a big gray coat skulking around the woods. Something about him just didn't seem right. Not five minutes later, a great black bird flew right up to him.

"And then it started speaking with a woman's voice! I reckon that feller was one of them nasty alchemists, and he'd done turned some poor lady into a bird. I ran to find the constable before he could do the same to me. But before I left, I heard what the bird said to him. And I figure, maybe it was a message from the airship."

"What did the bird say?" Greta doubted very much the bird was really an enchanted human, but if Kit's clever tinkering could put a tiny gramophone into a mechanical sparrow, then perhaps something similar could be used to send a message.

"Something about a little rock. And something about boring us."

"What direction were they heading?" Greta had no idea what the second half of that message meant, but she was fairly sure the first half meant the airship was headed to the city of Little Rock.

"Followed the river south, best I could tell." If they were headed to Little Rock, they'd have started out in that direction.

Greta stared off into the distance, as if she could bring the airship back with Kit by sheer force of will. "He's my dearest friend. I have to find him!"

The old woman gripped her arm, casting another anxious glance at the police officer. "The constable asked me to keep you here. I believe he just wants to ask you some questions, but this whole mess is too strange for my taste. If you wanna get outta here, I don't blame you. You run off, and when the constable comes round, I'll say I did my best."

A moment later, Greta was running through the woods. The constable gave a half-hearted chase, but he was old, overweight, and encumbered by the crowd. She wondered if he didn't really want to know what had happened, since it would probably mean more paperwork than the dragon had involved. She lost him among the trees and doubled back for home.

Back in the alley, her mind raced. She ran into the root cellar, where she stored most of her supplies. The cool cellar kept them better. She'd have preferred to have had her laboratory there, but her parents were adamant she not perform her experiments within the house. After this morning, she had to admit they had a point.

She grabbed some supplies and ran to Kit's workshop. His devices sold very quickly the past few months. Only the decorations from the Great Christmas Exposition remained. Clockwork angels, like the songbirds he made for her, could fly around on shimmering copper wings playing Christmas carols on gleaming brass harps.

A full-sized, steam-powered Santa sleigh with four clockwork reindeer sat in the corner. But it was built for show, not for speed. The locomotive tracks were only intended to move it short distances, mainly for loading onto and off a wagon. The only way it could carry her fast enough to catch up to Kit would be if it really could fly.

She looked at her alchemical supplies, and at the candles and lamps on Kit's work table.

Kit would kill her if she blew up his workshop.

But he was in no position to argue. He might be in terrible danger. As outlandish as the old woman's story had been, she believed it. Otherwise, the old woman was a muttering madwoman and there wasn't any hope Kit was still alive. Greta refused to accept that possibility. She sat her work box down, pulled out the components of the featherfall formulae and prayed the third time was a charm.

She was so absorbed in the task at hand, she didn't notice the pale, sharp-featured face peering in at her through the window of Kit's workshop, nor see the black bird flying away.

CHAPTER 6
MAKING THINGS CLEAR

Kit reclined in the padded velvet seat of the airship. A vague, insistent concern tugged at the back of his mind. The shadow of a thought plagued him. He had forgotten something of utmost importance. When he tried remembering what it might be, fear and confusion chilled him to the bone. When he stopped trying to remember, a warm, comforting calm descended upon him like a fur robe.

He had no memory of how he'd come to be in the luxurious airship, seated across from a beautiful woman dressed in blue. His mind pulled forth images of plans, schematics, and the inner workings of a hundred mechanical devices. He knew his name, and that he resided in the city of St. Louis in the Republic of Missouri. But the information was divorced from any personal recollection. It was as if his brain were a Lovelace engine, which someone had fed a stack of punch cards. For a moment, he looked down at his hands, just to confirm he was a flesh and blood man, not an automaton.

On some level, he knew this should be upsetting, but he didn't feel the slightest bit troubled. On the contrary, he felt an extraordinary confidence. His mind felt sharp, focused and clear, as if he could solve any problem set before him. Neither the chilly gondola nor his torn, muddy clothing bothered him.

He felt nothing. He remembered nothing. But he could imagine anything.

He wondered how he'd gotten so dirty. He pursued the question with his crystal-clear mind, which called forth an image of being chased by mechanical wolves. It was the closest he could come to a real memory, although even that seemed like something which had happened to someone else.

He strained to recollect anything at all prior to their pursuit, but he was overwhelmed with a barrage of foreboding images of fear, failure, and futility. When he quit trying to remember, his calm and clarity returned. As long as he remained focused on the present, he felt powerful and capable.

The only thing which continued to disturb him was a nagging sense he'd been interrupted in the middle of something vitally important. Something which he must finish at all costs. But he had no idea what that thing might be.

✳ ✳ ✳

Evelyn DeWinter watched as the young man

coughed and blinked, gripping the padded leather seat of the Aeolus as the airship gondola swayed in the light wind. The soft whirr of its propellers nearly covered the quiet thrum of the engines. With a pale blue and white color scheme, and a steam engine created to run almost soundlessly, the Aeolus could pass through the skies practically unnoticed.

In the opposite seat, Evelyn regarded her passenger with a cool and calculating gaze, before her features shifted into a mask of troubled concern. There was still plenty of time to divest herself of the tinker if he proved troublesome.

A groan brought her attention back to her disheveled passenger. "Ah, there you are, Mr. Merryweather. I'm relieved to see you coming around."

He looked at her in unguarded surprise. "How do you know my name?"

"Because, by a remarkable coincidence, I was on my way to St. Louis to make you an offer of employment when I discovered you dangling above the Mississippi. Imagine my surprise when the poor soul my Captain Guthrie spotted turned out to be the very man I had traveled here to meet." She smiled at Kit, but the smile didn't reach her eyes. She studied him, gauging his reaction.

"That is quite a coincidence indeed, ma'am." A look of pained confusion crossed his face. "I'm afraid you have me at a loss. I assure you, I'm very grateful for your assistance. But I don't know who you are, and it seems you know more about me than I do." He frowned, shaking his head slowly. "Aside from my name, I can't seem to remember much about who I am, or how I came to be here."

She graced him with a dazzling distant smile. "Oh, my goodness! Well, it's not uncommon for people who've been struck in the head to have some memory difficulties for a short while. Perhaps you were injured as you fell? Tell me, what exactly do you remember?"

His eyes scanned the polished floorboards of the Aeolus, as if he expected to find his memories scattered across their surface. "It's the strangest thing. My head is full of information. My name. Blueprints. Schematics. There's knowledge aplenty, but of memories . . . I can find almost nothing."

"I'm not at all surprised to hear your mind is full of mechanical information. That is why I sought you out. You've become quite notable for your engineering work these past months, Mr. Merryweather."

She lifted a stack of newspaper clippings on a small rosewood table next to the velvet bench and showed them to him. A halftone photograph graced the top clipping. It showed a man dressed as Saint Nick standing next to a steam-powered sleigh and four mechanical reindeer. The headline blared "Mechanical Marvels! Christmas Exposition Huge Success!"

The dirty young mechanic sitting across from

her was visible in the background, leaning down to adjust something near the bottom of the sleigh. A gawky young girl fussed next to him. She had seen the girl in many of the photos. Her most trusted agent, Gresham, reported the two were practically inseparable. He'd been observing them for the past week, reporting via one of the clockwork ravens she used for secret communication.

She addressed the tinker again. "Are you sure you remember nothing of your past? How terrible!"

He shook his head slowly. "I recall being chased by some automata in the shape of wolves, and I think I vaguely recall being pulled aboard your fine ship. Beyond that? Nothing. Absolutely nothing."

Distress was etched across his handsome features, although it appeared softened by the numbing effects of the alchemical powder. Panic was a common side effect she'd encountered when using the powder to suppress a person's memory, so she'd adjusted the formulae to include a soporific compound.

It made the subject marvelously malleable.

Evelyn lowered her head, guarding her expression. She feigned horror. "Mechanical wolves! How awful. It sounds as if your success has attracted the attention of some terrible enemies."

Merryweather's eyes widened as he considered that possibility. "Do you really think those creatures might have been set after me in particular? Who on earth would want to do such a thing?"

"I think you underestimate your value."

"And I think perhaps you overestimate it, ma'am." He looked down at his grubby clothing and oil-stained fingers. "Granted, I have no mirror, but nothing about my appearance says I'm a person of much consequence."

Evelyn did her best to hide her disgust at his appearance. She wished the wolves hadn't necessitated hauling a common tradesman, coated in mud, onto the deck of her favorite and fastest airship. She'd have to order it scrubbed out when they landed.

"Not everyone values the skill to create clockwork and steam powered wonders, my dear. That doesn't mean those who possess it lack value. Oh, how rude of me. I suppose you're wondering who I am? Or where we're going?"

"We're moving due south," the young man replied. "I would guess at approximately 30 miles per hour. At this speed, we'll reach the Arkansas border within hours."

"Very good, Christopher. Or is it Kit? I believe the papers said you prefer the latter." She was curious to see more precisely how the formulae had affected him. Did he even remember what he preferred to be called? His reasoning faculties seemed undiminished. He'd made that calculation with startling speed. Of course, if he hadn't been somewhat remarkable, she wouldn't have chosen him.

"You may call me whatever you like, madam."
The gleam of alchemical enchantment shone in his
eyes as he gazed at her through spectacles flecked
with dirt.

Perfect.

He was bound to her will now. The formulae
would ensure he did anything she asked of him.
Like a machine, every soul had a key, a means of
control. Her formulae found that key and
transferred ownership to her.

"Kit, allow me to introduce myself. My name
is Evelyn DeWinter. Like you, I believe the papers
sometimes refer to me by something other than my
given name."

"They call you the Snow Queen."

Evelyn smirked at the soubriquet. It had been
intended as an insult, devised by a journalist who
was angry over her refusal to let him publish her
photograph. The pushy little twerp had no idea what
it was like to grow up in the public eye.

As the only child of wealthy industrialist
Robert Alva DeWinter, Evelyn was a celebrated
heiress. She had little enough privacy, and no
intention of giving up her ability to travel without
being recognized. She'd refused to take umbrage
at the offense. Instead, she'd made every effort to
live up to the name. If he wanted to characterize
her as cold, regal and remote, then nobody could
complain of surprise when that's exactly how she
behaved.

"I see you have heard of me." She laughed, a brittle, tinkly sound even to her own ears. "Tell me, how does reality compare with my formidable reputation?"

"I can't imagine the opinion of a poor tinker would matter to you. Or what use you'd have for me. Not that I mind. I'd happily sit here and stare at you for hours, if that's all you require."

"I'm afraid I require a great deal more of you, Kit. But I promise you'll be richly rewarded for your work. Please, I must insist you return with me to Little Rock, at least until you recover your personal memories. We can also investigate the source of the wolves. I fear for your safety otherwise, wandering around alone with no recollection of your own past."

"So we are going to Arkansas, then?"

Evelyn smiled at the word "we." He had already acquiesced to traveling out of his home republic, and showed no sign of questioning her outlandish story.

"I have interests I must inquire about, including a gold mine in the Ouachita Mountains. My business in Little Rock pertains to the reason I require your assistance. Did you know, in addition to its value as currency, gold is a useful element in advanced alchemical processes?"

"Yes, I'm aware of that fact." A troubled frown crossed his face, and he winced in pain for a few moments before the expression turned blank.

Ah, the girl. He must have learned something of alchemy from her. He must have been quite attached to her. The powder's effect intensified whenever the subject experienced powerful emotions.

When Gresham had sent the raven messenger saying the boy was headed towards the park alone, she'd seized the opportunity. Her original plan had been to leave evidence the two had run off together. Now she didn't have to deal with the messy business of eliminating the girl. Her plans were too close to fruition to take any unnecessary risks.

Gresham had loosed the wolves and they'd driven the boy to the river just as planned. These models were a vast improvement over her prototype, but the new wolves were a little more vicious than she'd anticipated. They were supposed to keep the tinker at bay near the river's edge, not run him over it.

Good thing the young man had been smart and agile enough to get to the branch, and her pilot Guthrie had the brains to improvise with the harpoon. Fishing the tinker out of the river would have made an even bigger mess of the Aeolus.

She would need to send a message back to Gresham to make sure her ruse had succeeded. After that, she needed him to travel to the Boreas, her flagship zeppelin anchored in the Kentucky republic. She wanted assurances that the Pineville mine had produced the necessary amount of alchemical coal. If all went well, she would be traveling there soon.

She pulled a small wooden case with ornate carving and polished brass fittings from beneath the bench. Placing it on her lap, she popped the latches open to reveal a padded interior lined with royal blue velvet, in which lay two black-painted clockwork ravens. She lifted one from the case, squeezing the wings against the body to activate it.

A homing device would seek out the nearest of several rings she'd created for her various agents, before returning home to the case which was almost always with her.

Evelyn spoke in crisp, clear tones. "I've met with our friend. Returning to Little Rock. Go ahead to the Boreas." She released the raven and it flew off to deliver her message. With any luck, it would be awaiting her with his confirmation when they arrived in Arkansas. The tin birds were breathtakingly swift flyers.

"What a curious device." The dull tone of Kit's response seemed at odds with the interest implied by his words.

"Yes, isn't it, though? I find that, as a woman of enterprise, I have made a few enemies of my own. Some who might even bribe or threaten an aetherwire telegraph operator, if they thought they could divine my business plans from my messages. So I devised these. They're difficult to spot, and a bit more precise than a telegram."

* ❄ *

Evelyn craved precision in everything, but most especially in the things — or people — she viewed as tools. After the mishap at the cliff, she would need to adjust the formulae that bound the wolves' spirits to the machinery. Their aggressive pursuit was far too close to exhibiting a will of their own, and could have been disastrous. They were a unique hybrid of alchemy, mechanics and an ancient Mesopotamian means of creating an artificial construct, called a golem.

Her mysterious new mentor, Valentine, had introduced her to the long-forbidden Eastern science of enchantment. He'd warned her they'd need very precise instructions. Their agility was an advantage, but she needed to be able to control them better. Much like Valentine, whom she had a frustrating lack of control over. Trusting a renegade alchemist was a dodgy business, but the alchemical theories she'd learned were worth it.

The young man sitting across from her was also a tool she needed to be able to control. Tedious as she found small talk, it would be best to gauge the effects of the powder before they landed. She favored him with a smile.

"Once my business in Little Rock is concluded, we'll proceed to another of my holdings in the Republic of Kentucky, where I require your help with a matter of great importance."

His glassy, devoted gaze, under the influence of the formulae, reassured her that she had him under complete control. Of course, the best way to test that control was to give him a reason to reject her, and see how he reacted.

"I suppose you've also heard the rumors about me, then? About how my father died under mysterious circumstance? The whispers and insinuations from the former owners of the businesses I've acquired since taking over their companies?"

As that rarest of creatures, a beautiful heiress, the newspapers had expected her to dominate the society pages with a brilliant match, marrying a man to run her father's empire. They'd licked their lips at the prospect of issues filled with photographs of the infamous Snow Queen wearing the latest fashion at one ball or cotillion after another. Instead, she'd snubbed the eligible bachelors who tried to curry favor, and not only retained control of her father's business, but expanded it considerably.

The establishment was not amused.

"I'm sure those stories were just the rantings of jealous and desperate men."

Undoubtedly. Even if they *were* all true.

She shifted position, her spine still poker-straight. "You're sure, Kit? Let me tell you the truth, then. I'm considered the wealthiest woman alive. My financial holdings exceed those of all but a handful of the world's richest men. I'm also considered a great beauty. With that beauty, I've expanded my father's enterprise beyond even his wildest dreams. My wealth has been a lure, and my face has been a disguise."

Her satisfied smile didn't quite reach her crystal blue eyes.

"While businessmen plotted betrothals to steal my freedom and fortune, I quietly amassed control of their interests. At times, I've had to employ quite *aggressive* means to persuade a few stubborn souls. I hold no affection or pity, and that has been a greater power than my wealth or my beauty."

Kit's brown eyes continued to glow with artificial affection, giving them a striking greenish cast. The powder held him tight in its grip. She could probably confess to cold-blooded murder, and he would still adore and obey her, justifying it to himself in some broken loop of logic. While it was an effect she'd engineered, it never failed to fascinate her.

She supposed it was much like real infatuation, although she couldn't say from personal experience.

"I may be immune to love or pity, but not time and mortality. I hold considerable power, but it's not absolute. For five years, I've been putting a plan in motion to resolve these limitations. The answer is a machine no man has ever dared create. Now, with the help of a mentor and your assistance, I am close to achieving my aim."

She beamed at him with fierce, terrible joy. "The

ancient alchemists had it backwards. They changed course, believing alchemy existed to bring technology to its apex. They abandoned the search for the philosopher's stone just when the answer stood right before them! Technology was the missing element! Fools! My machine employs modern engineering to achieve the true, original purpose of the alchemists, and it's nearly finished. It only needs a skilled mechanic to calibrate it and correct a few lingering design flaws."

"You have my skills at your disposal." He seemed pleased at the chance to help her, but she hadn't yet revealed the cost. She wondered if his enthusiasm would wane when he discovered the chain reaction she intended to set in motion.

"According to what I've read in the papers, you're a perfect choice, Kit. Not only a tinker skilled enough to finish my machine, you're still at the beginning of what I'm sure will be a glorious and prosperous career. An engineer who was already prominent would have been far harder to secure, and even more difficult to keep."

"What's this machine you need me to finish?" Kit asked.

"I call it the Eternity Engine. It will grant me an eternity of youth, beauty, and power. Can you imagine it?"

She leaned forward, gripping his dirty hand in her pristine white-gloved one. "Once I possess that power, the world will be in the palm of my hand! I can demand anything, from anyone, in exchange for eternal life. I'll unite the republics, end these squabbling civil wars, and create a continental empire under my wise and everlasting rule." She smiled in satisfaction, leaning back deeply into the plush seat.

"There would be a long and bloody rebellion against any overthrow of democracy," said Kit. "The republics have rejected unified rule since the revolution. You'd need more mercenaries than there are men to create such an empire."

Through the effect of the alchemical powder, she could see a mounting distress rise in his expression. His eyes flashed their natural dark brown for a moment. It seemed she had reached the limit of the powder's ability to nullify his reason and manipulate his emotions.

The young tinker's will was stronger than she'd anticipated. If it wore off this quickly, she might need to adjust the formulae's strength. Kit blinked and shook his head. He winced, gripping the sides of his head as the powder induced a state of terror and panic. The effect occurred whenever the powder was wearing off, disabling any subject under its control until she could administer another dose.

She shook a handful of the powder from her reticule and blew it into his face. He screamed in agony, writhing as the sharp particles worked their way into his eyes and sinuses, dissolving to find the fastest possible path to his brain.

Moments later, he was her docile, adoring admirer again.

CHAPTER 7
FLIGHT PLAN

Greta stared hard at the three bottles of luminescent blue formulae on the table. After breaking into her emergency savings, a frantic visit to the herbiary, an apothecary supply store, and several trips to her stash of supplies in the cellar had yielded enough ingredients and equipment for a triple batch of featherfall.

She shuddered to think what a miscalculation like the one she'd made this morning would have done to a batch this large. Turned St. Louis into a floating city?

But she hadn't miscalculated. Not with Kit's life at stake. She'd remained calm, focused on the task at hand, and completed the formulae in record time. A small sample worked perfectly on a wooden mallet, a cast-iron poker and three horseshoes, all of which floated around the workshop like toy boats bobbing slowly across the surface of a pond. A splash of water had brought them tumbling to the ground.

As long as it doesn't rain, this just might work.

It should have been a moment of triumph, but she could hardly enjoy it. She was still too far away from catching up to whomever had kidnapped Kit.

Hope had welled up in her heart after realizing she could use featherfall to turn the Christmas exposition sleigh into a makeshift airship. Then, as always, reality had descended with a crashing thud. She needed more than an idea, she needed a plan, and Kit was the planner. She could come up with wild ideas and inspiration easily enough, but when faced with basic problem solving, she tended to overlook where things could go wrong.

What would Kit do in this situation?

In her head, she could hear his calm, deep voice say "Contact the authorities."

No good. No time for that. What would I talk Kit into doing if he were here?

Untroubled by the logical inconsistency of Kit helping to plan his own rescue, she imagined him near, asking the questions he always asked and providing the rational suggestions he always provided. In short order, she'd come up with a reasonable plan. The real Kit could be fairly predictable, which made it easier to figure out what advice pretend Kit should give.

If she was going to rescue him, she'd have to do more than get the sleigh into the air. She'd need to do so without anyone noticing and reporting her. The Alchemists Guild may have had no restrictions on creating an air buoyancy formulae, but she suspected the Continental Commission on Air Traffic as well as the Aeronautic Navy of Missouri might take exception to a young lady flying an experimental aircraft over the republics at high speed.

And she intended to fly at as high a rate of speed as she could coax out of the machine. Time was wasting, and every moment carried her best friend further away and possibly into greater peril.

After that, the problems were considerably easier to solve. She could hardly take off from the alley without attracting unwanted attention, especially after the events of the day. This necessitated a tedious trip down the back alleys, driving the sleigh on its locomotive tracks, to the park. She kept one eye trained nervously on the windows of the houses, trying to come up with a plausible explanation for why she was driving a Christmas exhibit through the back streets of town after dusk in March.

After the day's earlier exploits, they must not have found her current adventure all that peculiar or interesting. Not a soul came out to confront her. Once she'd gotten to the park, she made haste to reconfigure the steam engine's gears to the propellers she'd cobbled together and apply and activate the featherfall formulae before the constable stumbled upon her activities.

She doused the surface of the sleigh with the first bottle of featherfall. Then she pulled out a torch from her box of supplies and lit it from the lantern she'd brought along. She brushed the edges of the flames against the sides of the sleigh, like a painter putting a final coat of shellac on her work.

By the time she had heated the reindeer and the front edge of the sleigh, it was rising up from the ground. Greta suppressed a squeal of excitement and relief.

It was working!

She tossed her supplies into the sleigh, and clambered up into it. From inside, she swept the torch all around the outside and inside of the conveyance. With every pass, it floated higher and higher, till she cleared the treetops.

With a great whoop of triumph, she fired up the engine and set the propellers spinning. The sleigh shot forward, causing her to tumble over the driver's seat into the cargo area which had held Santa's enormous bag of toys. She pulled herself back up and dragged herself back into what was now the pilot's chair. Her gloved hands worked the controls, and she quickly figured out how to direct the makeshift airship, although it didn't turn with anything like precision.

After some consternation about whether to leave them behind, she'd left the clockwork reindeer attached to the sleigh, thinking they made the bizarre contraption look a bit more natural. It turned out to be a good instinct; they helped steer the thing like a forward-mounted rudder, prancing across the night sky. She rejoiced that she'd decided to activate them first. Climbing across them with the torch while hanging in midair might have been a strain on even her nerves.

Greta slowed the propellers slightly and reached under the seat for the old blankets and scarves she'd need to bundle herself up against the cold, pulling her goggles over her eyes and wrapping a scarf around her face to protect her from the bracing wind. Her workbox and the angel decorations rattled against the floorboards.

She scanned the air, looking for the landmarks and airship lightposts which would guide her way to Little Rock, where she hoped the captors had taken Kit. She was gratified to see a beacon in the distance to the south.

She would follow their trail towards the Arkansas border. Greta feared her flying sleigh could not overtake the expensive airship the old woman from the park described. She had another outrageous idea to speed her progress.

Once, when she'd been working in the lab, a particularly volatile mixture had caught fire. Jets of flame from the top of the bottle had propelled it across the room like the Chinese rockets she had seen during a fireworks display.

Dare I attempt another successful formulae in one day? Especially when the next is a controlled explosion?

Although she had far more experience creating explosions than any of the other achievements she'd accomplished today, she decided she didn't like her odds of success. She had cheated death enough times for one day. If the rockets misfired, it might destroy her air-sleigh. Kit would be lost for certain.

As she soared through the Missouri sky, she wondered who on earth could have taken him. The most obvious reason was someone needed his mechanical skills, and had seen the newspaper articles from the exposition. She agreed with the old woman from the park: anyone with a personal airship must be wealthy. At least, it implied someone with means enough to just hire a simple tinker as opposed to kidnapping him.

The abduction cast a grim light on the whole affair. Whomever was responsible either expected Kit to refuse to do whatever work was required, or didn't intend to let him walk away after it was completed.

Most likely, both.

She diverted from the glowing trail of beacons as she neared the Arkansas border. Slipping a flying Santa sleigh pulled by four copper reindeer past the border unnoticed would work better away from the main roads and airship routes. She'd make camp and sleep in the woods.

A small airship was not made for overnight travel. They'd most likely stop in the capital city of Little Rock several miles past the border, at least for the night. Even as large as the city was, it only had one sky port. She'd pick up the chase the next day.

She found an empty swath of grass in the woods near the edge of the city, and poured a bucket of water down the sides of the sleigh. It slowly dropped to the ground, landing with a jarring bump. Switching the gear configuration, she drove the sleigh into the edge of the woods, and covered it with brush and leafy branches. The shiny copper reindeer were the most difficult to hide. After a few minutes, she made a bedroll on the ground, and built a small fire.

The sound of coyotes in the distance sent a chill down her spine.

Proper young ladies were most definitely not supposed to sleep outdoors, much less alone. Her parents would be appalled if they ever found out. Hopefully, she would be able to return home before they did. As she buried herself under the blankets and stared into the flickering fire, she allowed herself to consider a possibility she hadn't earlier.

What if Kit had left willingly? What if the owner of the airship had made him an offer he wanted to accept, albeit under unusual and suspicious circumstances?

Surely he wouldn't have run off without letting her know what was going on. Of course, her parents, for all their consternation with her usual improprieties, would probably be equally certain she'd never run off alone without leaving so much as a note of explanation. And she had just insulted him terribly. Not to mention nearly gotten him killed. Again.

Maybe the airship owner had offered him a lucrative job, and he'd finally decided he'd had enough of Greta and her shenanigans. Could she really blame him?

As she drifted off to sleep, her final thought was if that was true, she was going to kill him for making her worry like this.

CHAPTER 8
LOOSE ENDS

The Little Rock skyport stood like a ragged sentinel against the setting sun. The tower of iron and brass scrollwork jutted into the purple sky, ringed with platforms dotted with airships of every size and description. A vibrant patchwork of balloons and sails of every color swayed in the breeze like a field of heavy-headed wildflowers, despite the huge canvas wind breaks.

One central shaft carried the steam lift, an ingenious contraption which ferried passengers, cargo and crew from the upper platforms down to the street. Open stairwells spiraled to the ground around it, like arteries through which a stream of people and goods surged into and out of the Republic of Arkansas.

Missouri was a trade center as the gateway to the western nations. Arkansas' wealth came from an abundance of natural steam power. The early settlers had discovered the hot springs and built great steamworks to power factories. They constructed steam gardens, hothouse conservatories which grew exotic and ordinary crops year round for export to nearby republics.

Arkansas had quickly earned a reputation for luxury and excess. Little Rock was one of the most cosmopolitan cities west of the Mississippi. It lacked the patina of age and respectability New York or Boston possessed, but it made up for it with an adventurous spirit — and a total absence of propriety.

The Aeolus docked at the skyport on one of the smaller platforms near the ground. These required greater skill to navigate, but Guthrie was a fine pilot and managed it easily. Evelyn instructed Kit to follow the pilot down to the street. He nodded, his handsome young face unreadable.

The skyport bustled as always, but this platform only held four ships. Fewer people to notice her arrivals and departures, and all of them cheap when it came to to buying silence and forgetfulness. Most of them were anxious to avoid notice themselves.

A brown-haired man of about thirty years was securing a small cargo freighter nearby. The name Whirlwind was emblazoned on the side of his battered airship in lurid orange and gold script. Evelyn thought it a peculiar name. Tornadoes were the worst thing one could encounter in the air.

"Do you have the full docking fee, Elias? Or do you think you can win it off me in another poker game?" The port manager's tone indicated a long and friendly acquaintance. He slapped the younger man on the back.

"Here it is, you old rascal. But if you're foolish enough to sit down with me for a few hands, I'll gladly take it back from you." The rough voice bespoke a man who spent his days in the open wind and his nights throwing back cheap whiskey. Evelyn sneered at the pair from the shadows of the Aeolus. She'd been hoping the platform would be empty.

A porter ran breathlessly up to Evelyn from the office. "Miss DeWinter! I'm so sorry, I must have lost you against the sky. That new paint job and balloon are a bit hazardous. Could cause a collision."

At this, the port manager and the captain of the Whirlwind turned to look their way.

She frowned at the impertinent porter. "I assure you, my captain is quite skilled enough to avoid any such thing. If your vision is so poor it impedes your duties, perhaps you should consider a new line of work." She glared down her nose at the man.

The porter stuttered an apology, and picked up the small leather trunk she'd brought on the short trip to St. Louis. As he reached for the wooden case which held her clockwork ravens, she rapped him sharply on the knuckles.

"I will carry that one."

As she paid the startled porter, she noticed the raven she'd released earlier alight in the stairwell leading down to the steam lift.

"Please take the trunk ahead. I have some business to discuss with the port manager." The porter nodded and began carting the trunk down the stairs. She stepped back onto the Aeolus, pretending to fuss with something in the gondola until the porter was out of sight.

She carried the wooden case to the stairwell and bent low, swishing her azure skirts out of the way to pick up the mechanical bird. Holding it close to her face, she pressed its wings tight against its body. A whirring and clicking emanated from the creature, followed by a hollow, wheedling voice.

"The girl knows the tinker lives. The airship was seen. Should I take care of her?"

Evelyn's face turned white. She regained her composure just before she crushed the raven in her grip. She pulled a piece of alchemical coal from the case, feeding it to the bird like a morsel of corn. She pressed its wings down again and recited another message.

"The girl is no threat. Leave her to me. Proceed to the Boreas."

Unlike the wolves, Gresham was a tool she controlled with absolute precision. Quiet and pale as death, the thin man was perfectly obedient. If a warm heart beat beneath his charcoal suit, she'd seen no evidence of it while he'd been in her employment. He was a monster, but one who seemed to relish being under the control of someone else.

In short, he suited her needs precisely.

Much as he would enjoy eliminating the girl, he would do nothing without Evelyn's express permission. She released the bird, which flew north towards the invisible pull of Gresham's ring.

Just as she snapped the case closed, a shadow fell across the stairwell. The port manager and the young freighter captain stared at her.

"Do you need some assistance, ma'am? I could have sworn I heard voices." The port manager's bushy mustache twitched. He'd never seemed to like her, although, like everyone, he treated her with cautious respect.

"I'm perfectly fine. As you can see, there's no one else here."

"Odd that we both heard someone." The captain of the Whirlwind had the weathered face of a sailor to match his raspy voice.

"The docking platform has many levels and airship balloons have peculiar acoustic properties. Sound carries strangely." She glared at the men, daring them to contradict her.

The freighter captain looked at the Aeolus, then gave the wooden case a speculative gaze. "Lots of things being carried strangely this evening."

❄ ❄ ❄

"My apologies, Miss DeWinter. I wasn't certain where you'd want me to seat your . . . guest." The carriage driver looked significantly at Kit's filthy clothing and the pristine brocade which covered the seats of the carriage.

"Sit him up front with you." Evelyn sighed. Another little detail failed to go according to the plan. It was inconceivable that anyone would recognize the tinker during the short drive to her town house, but these small hitches were accumulating at an alarming rate.

Evelyn seethed in her carriage. She hated it when even the tiniest details failed to follow her schemes. The tinker was supposed to have been plucked from the edge of the cliff, not scraped off its muddy side. They were supposed to have escaped any notice when landing. Everyone was supposed to have believed Kit died in the river.

If there was one thing Valentine harped on, it was to never leave loose ends. He certainly abided by that rule himself. He'd spilled the secrets of forbidden alchemy as if sharing a recipe for strawberry scones, but he'd never offered his last name. She doubted Valentine was really his given name. His insights into alchemy had been indispensable, especially his suggestions for avoiding the interference of the Guild. His motives were far less clear. The last thing she needed was for him to decide she was a loose end which needed snipping.

She'd meant what she said when she told Gresham the girl was no threat. Still, it was possible she could show up looking for the tinker.

This was not the time for inconvenient questions from what passed for the authorities in Little Rock.

If the girl from the newspaper stories was anything like Kit, she might be more formidable than she first appeared. According to Gresham, she was an amateur alchemist, a girl of good breeding but poor manners. Evelyn hadn't attained her position by allowing even harmless opponents any quarter.

The carriage chugged to a stop in front of the impressive stone facade of her town house. Kit clambered down from the front and followed her as obediently as a puppy. The door was opened by Gaskon, her 'gen butler. He bowed as they entered, an action with more fluid grace than most men of flesh and blood could have accomplished.

"Welcome home, Miss DeWinter. Do you require anything?" The rich, warm tones of his voice always brought a shiver to Evelyn's heart. Whether that frisson was the thrill of getting away with illegal alchemy or a twinge of guilt was difficult to say. She chose to believe it was the former. Guilt was the one luxury she could never afford. Not if she truly intended to fulfill her destiny. She responded to the 'gen in her usual clipped tone.

"Send Richardson to the haberdashers. We'll need to replace Mr. Merryweather's clothes. His adventures have irreparably damaged them and we will be leaving for Pineville tomorrow morning." The Boreas was the only place she felt safe building the Eternity Engine.

"Very good. You've also received two wires."

Gaskon handed her two slips of paper, each imprinted with a neatly typed message. The first was from Valentine.

"Happy to see hounds working well. Anticipate progress report soon. If not, I may be obliged to pay a visit. - V"

The words sent a shiver down her spine wondering what Valentine meant by "paying a visit." She doubted he'd be stopping by for a cup of tea and pleasant conversation. The small man, with his suave accent and the wicked gleam in his eyes, emanated power and ruthless self-interest.

He was far too much like her.

The second telegram was from Gresham. It could not be good news. He wouldn't send a wire unless it were too urgent to wait for the raven to return.

"Girl in pursuit. Agent observing her. Should I intervene?"

Evelyn wadded the paper into a ball. An agent of the Alchemists Guild was involved? She drew a deep breath. The Guild getting wind of her plot defied probability. Even if they knew about the Engine, and had connected the tinker's disappearance to it, they couldn't have gotten an agent there this quickly. The Guild was a hopeless quagmire of bureaucracy, one of the many reasons she'd refused to join them.

No, most likely they were simply scouting the girl for membership. She was an alchemist, after all. But if she was an alchemist whose skill had attracted Guild attention, she'd need to be eliminated before she caused any more trouble.

Gresham would happily slit the girl's throat, but such obvious foul play would draw too much attention. No, Gresham should deal with the Guild's agent, and she'd handle the girl in a more delicate fashion. This far from St. Louis, even if the body was found, it was unlikely anyone would identify her. The Engine would be complete soon, and then it wouldn't matter.

"Gaskon, please send a wire to Gresham. He's probably still at the telegraph office awaiting a reply. The message should read 'Give my regards to our friend. I will prepare a reception for the young lady.'"

"Very well, ma'am. Will there be anything else?"

"Send the carriage for Halfacre," she said. "I have a job requiring her attention."

There was a slight pause before Gaskon nodded, and rolled from the room. Evelyn chewed her lower lip and narrowed her eyes, troubled by the 'gen's pause. She made a mental note to visit the basement and ensure everything there was as it should be.

Isadora Halfacre was the widow of Hiram, her steam factory foreman, and useful in delicate situations where more overt means of persuasion were impractical. Hiram had disappeared, presumed killed in a tragic accident some years back. A few weeks later, Gaskon had replaced Evelyn's former, far less capable automaton butler.

The Halfacres had no children or family, so the widow depended entirely upon Evelyn's generosity. She seemed harmless, even helpless, but she'd do the job. A few ounces of gold in the widow's pocket, a sprinkling of poison in a cup of tea, and this girl would be merely another obstacle overcome on Evelyn's path to absolute power.

CHAPTER 9
THE RUSTY SEXTANT

For the first time in her life, Greta wished she were better dressed. Her green poplin dress hadn't been terribly impressive even before getting rumpled from spending the night sleeping on the ground. She stood on the corner of two busy thoroughfares at the edge of Little Rock, the shining capital of Arkansas.

Even at this early hour, a mix of stylishly-dressed individuals and outlandish conveyances crowded the busy streets. Steam-driven bicycles weaved between heavy horse-drawn carriages. The new horseless carriages, a novelty in St. Louis, were here in abundance. Fashionable ladies strolled under parasols, protected from the chill by fur wraps or heavy velvet cloaks. Gentlemen ranged from dandies in frock coats to roguish frontiersmen in dusters and sturdy boots. Here and there, a revolver peeked out from a holster beneath a man's coat, pressed against a brocade vest.

Saloons offering every kind of pleasure and vice flourished alongside factories and hothouse gardens. It was a dangerous city for a young girl all alone. Or it would be, if the girl wasn't carrying a small incendiary device in her pinafore. Greta came to the city prepared for anything. In this case, prepared meant carrying alchemical explosives.

Greta wrapped her wool cloak around her tightly, and peered in every direction, hoping to catch a glimpse of Kit's familiar face. She trudged through the streets, trying her best not attract attention. Making her way to the skyport was an arduous process. At least it presented a landmark which was impossible to miss. The enormous tower soared above the streets, punctuated with platforms at various angles and degrees.

She reached the entry gate for the skyport, where a pair of brass sentinels stood at attention. A fashionable group of travelers approached, each person dropping a punch card ticket into a slot in the gate. A series of loud clicks and taps erupted from the gate, and one of the 'gens would open it and let the people pass.

She had no idea how to get past the automata. She didn't have a ticket for any of the passenger ships. A captain or crew member, even a delivery person, probably had a similar punch card to gain access.

As she puzzled over this problem, a loud noise attracted her attention.

"Elias Hamm, get out of this saloon! I never want to see your face again!" The sound of chairs being toppled erupted from the building to her right. A scuffle had broken out inside The Rusty Sextant.

Greta scuttled next to the door. A tavern this close to the skyport was surely frequented by airship crewmen. If she slipped inside during the fray, maybe she could sneak off with a punch card without being noticed. She wasn't going to steal it, just borrow it for a bit. After she knew where to start looking for Kit, she'd return it to the tavern owner, saying she'd found it on the boardwalk outside.

Before she could make it through the doors, they flung open. A scraggly-looking man with brown hair and dusty clothes bounced out, landing in a heap on the street. A steam-powered carriage bore down on the crumpled lump of humanity, by all appearances having every intention of rolling right over him. Greta gasped and grabbed his arms, trying to drag the poor man out of harm's way.

"Sir! You — ugh — need to get up!" she yelled at the man, who groaned and then lunged at her.

The steam carriage narrowly missed clipping his heels as he tumbled onto the boardwalk next to Greta. It chugged down the street, pouring smoke out of the stacks lined up along the back. The driver turned a moment to shake a fist at the both of them, yelling something rendered unintelligible by the noise of the machine and the crowds.

Up close, the man wasn't as old as he'd seemed at first glance. He had the weathered look of a sailor or airship captain, and he was in desperate need of a bath and shave. But he couldn't have been much over thirty.

"Are you all right?" Greta asked.

"Nope." The man spat blood into the street, revealing at least one missing tooth. "But at least I won't be nursing a set of broken ribs for the next few months." He looked her up and down, still sitting with skirts splayed out across the filthy sidewalk.

"You all right yourself, missy? I'm much obliged, but you're naught but a girl."

"At least I didn't end up tossed in the street like yesterday's refuse!" She patted her pinafore, relieved to discover the glass ampoules of explosive formulae still tucked securely inside. It was too early in the day for an unexpected detonation.

"Now, now, there! No need to take offense. Believe me, if anybody knows better than to underestimate the power of a scraggly young girl, it's me. You ain't the first one to pull me out of a bad scrape. You just don't seem the type to be wandering the streets of Little Rock alone." He coughed and spat again.

"Think you can get to your feet, Mister. . . ?"

"Captain. Hamm. Elias Hamm, of the airship Whirlwind. And yes, I think I can manage. I ain't got that much whiskey in me, and Prinny's boys didn't do that much damage before giving me the heave-ho."

Greta frowned at the rumpled and ragged

clothing. Airships were expensive, and he'd spoken with a pride that implied ownership.

"Should I have heard of this Whirlwind?" She scrambled to her own feet, and then helped pull Captain Hamm upright.

"The Whirlwind? It's the ship that made the Castille run in less than twelve days!"

Her blank stare was clearly not the response he'd hoped to elicit. Her indifference seemed to knock the wind out of him more than the toughs who'd kicked him out of The Rusty Sextant.

"Well, Captain Hamm, I don't suppose you'd be willing to do me a favor out of gratitude for having saved your life?"

"You didn't save my life. My ribs, maybe a broken leg."

"So you're not going to do me favor?"

"Depends. What's the favor, girl?"

"I need to get into the skyport."

"When? Why?"

"Right this minute, because my best friend has been kidnapped and the only clues to his whereabouts might be up there."

Captain Hamm glared at her for a moment, pressing his lips together as if considering what to say next.

"I can't get you in there right now, because I'd have to add you to my crew. And that would take a few days to get the paperwork run through. And before you ask, no, I'm not lending you my paperwork. Not that I don't trust you — which I don't — but it wouldn't do you no good anyhow. Even if the 'gens at the gate couldn't tell you're not me, you'd have to pass at least two human guards to get anywhere near the ships."

"But Captain, I need to find Kit! Every minute that passes means it's less likely I'll be able to catch up to whoever took him." Tears welled up in Greta's eyes. To be this close to a clue and have it pulled out from under her was unbearable.

"Now, hold on there, girl. I didn't say I wouldn't help you. I just said I couldn't get you into the skyport. If you tell me what you're looking for, I'll do the looking for you. I figure a broken rib is worth an hour or so of my time, at least."

Greta's eyes lit up with relief and joy. She flung her arms around Captain Hamm's neck. "You will? Oh, thank you, Captain! I can't thank you enough!" The man grunted and groaned a bit under her hug.

"Call me Elias. .So tell me, what is it I'm supposed to be looking for up there?"

"My friend was taken by someone in a small airship. A witness told me it was painted white and blue."

"Wait. You sure about that?"

"Pretty sure. The person didn't have any reason to lie, at least not that I know about."

"What's this Kit look like?"

"A bit taller than me. Strong and solid — he's a tinker. With black hair and brown eyes."

"He wouldn't have been covered in dirt the last time you saw him, would he?"

Greta's eyes widened in surprise. "He'd slid over a muddy embankment when he was captured. Captain . . . Elias, I mean . . . did you see him? Did you see the airship?"

Elias nodded slowly. "I believe I did. Grant you, I didn't get a good look at his face, but it sure sounds like the young man who stepped off a little zephyr ship that landed just after I did last night. And the ship's a match, for certain. Not too many flying with those colors. What was the name of that ship? Oriolus? Aurelius?"

"Elias, can you find out who owns that ship? Who else was on it?"

"It was a light crew. Just the man you're describing, the pilot and a woman."

"A woman?"

"Yeah. She was definitely the one in charge of the whole shebang. Seemed kind of shifty, too, although to be honest that isn't too out of the usual here.

"What about Kit? Could she have been holding a weapon on him? Did he seem in distress?"

Elias paused a moment, as if hesitant to tell her his first impression. "No. He didn't seem in any distress. To be honest, he looked sort of smitten with her."

Greta looked down just to be sure none of the thugs from The Rusty Sextant had snuck up and thrown a knife into her chest. Smitten? Kit was about to propose to her just yesterday afternoon, and by last night he was smitten with some stranger?

"Are you feeling well, girl? You look like you just got a mouthful of castor oil."

"I'm fine, Captain Elias. I'm sure there's more to this than meets the eye. Either way, I'm going to get to the bottom of it. Do you think the port manager would give you any more information?"

"Like who she is and where you might find her?" He grinned. "He owes me a little money. I'll run up right quick and see if he's willing to settle up with some information."

Greta nodded, and pointed at a coffee house just down the block. "Thank you again, Captain. If you don't mind, I think I'll wait for you in there."

The airship captain grinned at her. "That's a good idea, girlie. Hey, by the way, what's your name?"

"Greta. Greta Jane Singleton."

"Well, Greta, I'll see what I can find out and be back in a wink."

* * *

Greta had been stirring cream into the same cup of coffee for almost an hour before Captain Elias returned and found her. His words about Kit and the woman from the airship still felt like a lead plumb weight sitting uncomfortably in her stomach.

Of course, it wasn't as though she wanted Kit to be in love with her. She was still a mess, still unfit for matrimony, still a walking disaster. The worst thing she could do for him was accept the proposal she'd interrupted.

Then again, she had managed to formulate a working anti-gravity potion, pilot a flying Christmas decoration across two republics and rescue an errant airship captain from being crushed under a carriage, all within two days. Maybe she wasn't the unmitigated mess she'd always believed.

She told herself she wasn't jealous. She was just concerned, as any good friend should be under the circumstances. It wasn't at all like Kit to run off without letting anyone know. He was behaving strangely, and it was most likely this woman's fault. Once she was reassured that Kit was safe and in his right mind, he could elope with the next floozy to pass by, if he wanted.

Right after she kicked him in the shins.

The look on Elias' face when he returned made the plumb weight dig a little deeper into her gut.

"Didn't you find anything out?" She gripped the cup of coffee as she awaited his answer. Was she sure she even wanted to know what he'd discovered?

"I did. But it wasn't good. Have you ever heard of the Snow Queen?"

Greta searched her memory. The name sounded familiar, like something she should know. Snatches of stories she'd read in the newspaper sprang to mind.

"I think so. Isn't she some heiress or industrialist? Has something of an unscrupulous reputation?" She didn't mention the other thing she recalled, about how the Snow Queen was ravishingly beautiful and had broken the hearts of all the most eligible bachelors on the continent.

"That's the one. Her real name is Evelyn DeWinter. She's the woman from the airship last night."

With that, the plumb weight, and Greta's stomach, fell all the way to her feet.

"Kit's been taken by the Snow Queen?"

"He's definitely traveling with her. But by all signs he was there of his own free will. He was dirty as a pig, but he didn't seem injured." Elias gave her a sympathetic look as he slumped into the chair across from her. He waved at the man behind the counter, who sent a percolambulator to the table. The short cylindrical 'gen, with its domed top, rolled obediently over.

Burbling noise and fragrant steam poured out of the mechanical coffeepot. Elias grabbed a ceramic mug from the hooks which ringed the machine, and poured himself a cup. Greta refilled hers, adding a little more cream from the spigot on the side of the automaton.

"It took some convincing, but the port manager gave me this." He handed Greta a slip of paper with a scribbled street address.

She looked at the crumpled paper, her face

downcast. "Maybe she threatened him. Maybe he's putting on an act, trying to get her to lower her guard so he can escape." Even to her own ears, those explanations sounded like wishful thinking.

The airship captain threw her a dubious look. "Maybe. Or maybe your friend just stumbled into a good opportunity, and had to either take it or lose it on the spot. You say he's a tinker. Maybe the Snow Queen's airship was in the right place at the right time to help him out of a jam, and she liked the look of him."

Frowning, Greta's mind ran back to her assumptions when Kit had tried to propose. She'd been convinced some industrialist was going to take him away from her. Maybe she'd been correct, just a little premature. The acclaim he'd received from the Great Christmas Exposition did make him an attractive employee.

She gulped, trying very hard not to think about what else the Snow Queen might find attractive about Kit.

"You may be right, Captain. Maybe I'll find him, and he'll be on his way to send a telegram with nothing but good news. But I've known Kit since we were both children. If there's even a chance he's in danger, I need make sure he's safe. Heavens knows he's gotten me out of enough improbable scrapes over the years."

She sipped at her coffee, feeling her resolve return. "Thank you for all your help, Captain. I hope

I can return the favor someday."

Elias gave her a long thoughtful look. "Yep. You remind me of Mattie. One of my oldest friends, and a more loyal soul you'll never meet. You're quite a girl, Greta. I hope you find your friend, and he's fine as a frog's hair."

The airship captain gulped down his coffee, stood up and headed out to return to his own business. As he pushed through the doors, he looked at her over his shoulder, his eyes twinkling.

"But something tells me the Snow Queen's in for a mess of trouble when you find them, either way."

CHAPTER 10
LIES BENEATH

Isadora Halfacre crept nervously into Evelyn's parlor. The hour was late, but the old lady knew better than to hesitate when summoned.

She'd scraped her frazzled grey hair back into a bun beneath a black veiled hat. Her dress consisted of great swaths of fabric in blacks and muddy greys, still in mourning. Evelyn vaguely remembered her as she'd been when they first met, a plump matronly creature with fluttery hands and a high-pitched, girlish drawl. Widowhood had not been kind.

"Please come in, Mrs. Halfacre. Have a seat."

Evelyn gestured to an imposing wing-back chair. Instead of looking comfortable, or even regal, the odd angles and carvings made it resemble some Jacobean torture device. The mousy woman knew better than to risk offending her hostess. She gingerly planted herself on the chair's edge, leaning forward as if to listen attentively but actually to avoid having any more contact with the seat than absolutely necessary.

"You have some business for me, ma'am? Your

driver said it was of the utmost urgency." Fear radiated from the frail woman's frame.

"It is indeed important. As usual, it will require your diligent discretion. No one can know about this assignment." Evelyn shook loose the folds of her satin dress, smoothing the azure fabric across her knees. The widow's rumpled appearance disrupted her otherwise immaculately neat room. After she'd replaced her human servants with 'gens, Evelyn had grown accustomed to everything remaining frozen in a state of perfect order.

Particularly since creating Gaskon, the fewer nosy hirelings poking around the house in her absence, the better.

"What do you need, Miss DeWinter? You know I'm always at your disposal." Try as she might, the woman was unable to conceal an edge of bitterness to her tone.

"Do you know anything of my holdings in the Kentucky Republic?"

"Yes, Miss. If you recall, I helped you solicit the services of a number of tinkers and engineers for some project installed in your airship, the Boreas. How are Mr. Gunderson and Mr. Whitley getting along with their task, if I may ask?"

"I'm afraid not well at all." A frown crossed Evelyn's fine features. "Blunderson and Witless" as she'd dubbed them, had not worked out at all, in the end. To their great misfortune.

"I am sorry to hear that."

Not as sorry as they'd been. But that was not important at the moment.

"Don't worry. You couldn't have possibly known, and I've since found a most acceptable replacement. However, I find myself needing to confide in you to a greater degree than usual, to help you understand the gravity of the situation. Let us be entirely clear. The consequences of your breaking my confidence will be . . . dire."

She did not raise her voice, which maintained its light tone and musical cadence, but there could be no mistaking the open threat.

"Mrs. Halfacre, I believe I may speak candidly with you. I feel that we have an understanding, and that, unlike most people, you know me for who I am."

"I . . . I believe that's so, yes." The elderly woman was practically quivering, although whether it was from terror, suppressed rage, or a mixture of both was impossible to tell.

"The machine I've been building is called the Eternity Engine. It is the culmination of all my years of study in the science of alchemy. It will grant me untold power, and the gifts of the Philosopher's Stone. I will be able to turn back the hands of time, and turn lead into gold."

"That's wonderful news. I'm afraid I'm a little unclear as to what it might have to do with me, though." The woman was worrying the handle her leather satchel as if rubbing it would cause a genie to appear and whisk her away on a magic carpet. Unfortunately for her, the only carpet in view was Evelyn's very expensive rug.

"Well, there are a number of people who don't want to see me complete the Engine. It may have something to do with the fact that activating the device will result in a rather sudden and dramatic drop in both temperature and population." She offered Halfacre a wry smile, but the widow didn't return it. Instead, her mouth hung open in undisguised horror.

"What . . . whatever do you mean? Why on earth would that be necessary?"

Evelyn continue her tale. After years of plotting in secret, with no one knowing the full extent of her plans, it was intoxicating to speak them aloud. She considered it a foretaste of the freedom to do and say exactly as she pleased. It wasn't as if Halfacre had the will to oppose her, or if anyone would listen to the doddering old widow if she tried.

And she was so close. The Engine's completion was within her grasp, she knew it with absolute certainty. Kit would not fail her as the others had.

"Alchemical coal and steam start the engine to begin the process, but the final stage of the reaction requires a far greater power source. Perhaps you've heard of the recent research into solar power, capturing the energy of the sun itself? My device works on similar principles. It will drain a substantial amount of the heat contained within the earth's atmosphere.

"Doing so will cause a brief ice age of sorts for hundreds of miles when it reaches full power. The airship carrying it is heavily insulated, but those caught unprepared will likely die.

"I can assure you, many people will be quite unprepared."

A small incredulous squeak escaped Isadora Halfacre. "But, Miss DeWinter, that's murder! On a scale which boggles the mind." She attempted a nervous, half-hearted giggle. "Of course you're simply having fun at my expense. No sane person would ever do such a thing."

Silence filled the parlor for a long moment, before it was broken by a laugh like the sound of shattering crystal.

"Of course I'm joking, Mrs. Halfacre. Although to read what some of those awful newspaper reporters write about me, I'm sure it sounds almost plausible. You did seem quite distressed for a moment there." A hard, glittering-white smile spread across Evelyn's face.

Halfacre sucked in an enormous breath of relief. "You are quite a good actress, ma'am. If your business interests ever falter, you could consider a career on the stage. But in all earnestness, what is it you need me to do?"

"Nothing terribly demanding. I simply need you to delay a young girl."

A puzzled expression passed the widow's face. "Who do you need me to delay, and how?"

"The new tinker I've found has left behind his paramour in order to come work for me. She's a bit flighty and I'm afraid she'll prove to be a distraction. We're leaving for Pineville tomorrow, and I'm afraid she might come here and make a scene. I need you to intercept her. Bring her around to the Summer Garden. I'll have tea waiting with a harmless formulae to make her sleep. When she's unconscious, ring for my butler and leave. He'll take care of her."

"Your automaton will take care of her?"

"He'll watch over her until she wakes, which should be well after the tinker and I have left. I'm leaving an airship ticket for her to return home. Just make sure the girl takes the tea, ring for Gaskon, and leave. That's all."

"Well, that seems simple enough."

"Oh, and one last thing." Evelyn walked to a writing desk, and opened the wooden case which lay atop it. "I have been working on these." She pulled out one of the clockwork ravens. "They're quite ingenious little messengers. You simply squeeze the wings against the body, speak a short message and it flies to deliver it. I think they may be useful for those who can't read or write. Once you've taken care of the girl, if you would be so kind as to ease my mind?"

"Of course," said Halfacre, placing the black

bird gingerly into her satchel. But her guarded expression betrayed that her own mind was not at ease. Not at all.

✳ ❄ ✳

Kit shivered and looked around. He was surrounded by sparkling ice and snow. Gleaming blue-white scrollwork ornamented every surface in sight. The floor was chiseled into a parquet pattern of ice, rubbed rough enough to walk upon without slipping. A glittering frosty chandelier hung high overhead, shooting out prismatic beams of light in all directions.

How had he come to be here? This place was a palace, an enormous cavernous space. An urgent, anxious feeling anchored deep in his gut. There was something he needed to do, but he couldn't remember what it was. Something about "eternity."

Out of the corner of his eye, he caught a flash of blonde hair. He spun towards the image, just as the figure turned a corner. Had it been a pale platinum color, or a warm honey-gold? It had been too brief a glimpse to tell. He ran towards the retreating figure. He could hear the swish of skirts across the floor. A sense of panic gripped him.

You're going to lose her.

He picked up speed, desperate to catch up, his feet skittering on the slippery floor. He could hear the rhythmic clacking of boots ahead, but with every turn deeper into the labyrinth of the ice palace, the sound seemed further away.

Always tantalizingly out of reach.

Every so often, he could catch sight of a woman's skirt slipping around a corner. The weird, prismatic light bouncing off the layers upon layers of ice made the fabric appear blue to green to red and back again.

"Come back!" he shouted. "Please, don't go!"

His eyes, nose and throat burned from the cold.

A feminine voice called back. "Who are you looking for, Kit?"

He stopped in his tracks. He didn't know who he was chasing, or why.

* * *

A deep quiet settled over the town house. Halfacre had been dismissed and the mechanic lay asleep in the servants' quarters. Evelyn had no use for the rooms now. Gaskon and the other 'gens simply stopped moving, frozen into brass and steel statuary when they weren't needed.

The thought of Gaskon pinched her face with a frown. She was certain the 'gen had paused at the mention of Isadora Halfacre.

Evelyn chided herself. It couldn't possibly hurt just to slip down to the laboratory and ensure all was as it should be. There also the matter Valentine's pet project. He was as unpredictable as the weather, but his telegram meant he was anxious to hear if there had been any progress. She might as well reassure herself his grand idea was nothing but a fairy tale, concocted by an English madwoman.

She slipped through the twisting hallways of the enormous house, till she reached a door at the far western end. Gaskon had followed her, his usual silent movement rendered sinister by her own imagination.

"I don't require anything further tonight. Please return to the parlor." The automaton nodded, and retreated down the hallway. She opened the door, turned a dial to raise the flame on the gaslights, and headed down the twisting spiral staircase. Her laboratory looked just as she'd expected; still, cold and silent.

It was a very large room, much bigger than the original cellar had been. It had taken weeks of excavation, shoring up, and construction to expand it. But the effort and expense had been entirely worth it. Along one long wall lay rows of polished wooden cabinets, rather like caskets, although each had a round porthole of glass in the door. Copper pipes and black rubber hoses snaked around and through them, each covered with a thin layer of frost.

She approached the first cabinet, brushing the light glaze of ice from the porthole. Within the cabinet, she could see a large gray wolf. Every few moments, the beast's chest rose and fell. The breathing was much slower than normal, of course, but that was a result of the animus transferral process.

Just as Valentine's notes indicated, she'd been able to extract the animus from the wolf and bind it to her metal construct without killing it. The key was applying an alchemical formulae to induce a death-like sleep. Bringing the creature to the brink of death loosened the bonds between the body and animus.

She called her new creations animatons. The fashion of keeping clockwork pets was in vogue right now. People would pay large sums for realistic, lifelike creatures. As long as the Guild couldn't trace them back to her, it could be a lucrative new product.

Her heels clipped across the stone floor as she strode to the last of the cabinets. Beneath the glass lay the sleeping face of Hiram Halfacre, her erstwhile factory foreman.

This had been the next logical step in the process. Gresham had brought the man in, after rigging the pipe explosion so no one would be looking for him.

If he'd died in the process of creating the animaton, it would have been simple to slip his body back into the debris. But it hadn't killed him, no agents from the Guild had turned up, and now she had a perfect mechanical servant.

Valentine's interest in the experiment was more martial than commercial. The mad genius was convinced he could create an army of mechanicals. Evelyn's response had been conventional wisdom. It would take an army to capture and subdue enough men to animate an army. His reply had startled her.

He'd claimed he knew the secret to creating true artificial life: homunculi.

The artificial creatures had been mentioned in the legends of alchemy for centuries, but they were just that. A legend. No one could create life from nothing.

Valentine had produced a manuscript from an Englishwoman named Mary Shelley, the wife of the famous poet. It consisted of a collection of letters and correspondence which detailed a German scientist's attempt to reanimate a creature cobbled together from bits of corpses. Supposedly, he'd succeeded, although not without consequence.

"Electricity, my dear!" Valentine had exclaimed. "That is the source of the spark of life. That is what the traditional instructions for creating homunculi missed. Homunculi have small, fragile bodies. But imagine if we use the process you've perfected to capture the animus from hundreds of them. We could create a mechanical army, clever and agile as living men, who feel no pain, and cannot be stopped."

She had nodded along, but it was clear the idea was sheer folly. She'd agreed to perform some tests for him. He claimed to be a theoretical alchemist only, without a laboratory of his own. More likely, he preferred to let others take the risk of getting caught enacting his experiments. The tanks along the other wall of her laboratory were the result. Floating in the *aqua vitae* were a dozen tiny bodies, their features indefinite at this stage in the process and obscured by murky fluid.

Creating the mannikins, and getting them to a stage of development where they had recognizable features was simple. Now they remained in a vegetative state, floating in their tanks, unreactive to all but the most violent electrical stimuli.

She had tried to enervate the little beasties by electrifying the tanks with a steam-driven generator. Aside from some thrashing, nothing had come of it. In her opinion, if it were to work at all, it would require electricity of a wattage which could not be produced by anything less than a bolt of lightning. Unfortunately, one never knew when or where lightning would strike.

The homunculi had grown a bit in the week she had been away. Their features seemed infinitesimally sharper. Evelyn decided to give the generator another go. She put on her safety goggles, donned rubber gloves and threw the switch which would send an electrical current jolting through the copper pipes wound through the tanks.

Just as before, the little creatures twitched and thrashed, splashing fluid over the edges of the tanks. When she threw the switch back again, their movement stopped.

"Fool! These creatures are a waste of my time."

She pulled the gloves and goggles off, and

headed for the stairwell. Gaskon's power source was still safely ensconced in the cabinet. The alchemical seals appeared intact, and nothing could rouse their inhabitants while that remained the case.

While she was reassured nothing was amiss with Gaskon or the wolves, she worried about the lack of progress on the homunculi. She doubted Valentine would take failure gracefully, and this particular experiment could lead nowhere else.

It was essential Kit complete the Eternity Engine, and quickly. Once she had a weapon capable of eliminating huge swaths of people, Valentine's concerns would no longer be any of hers.

CHAPTER 11
DIGGING UP THE PAST

It didn't take long for Greta to find the home of Evelyn DeWinter, the infamous Snow Queen. As she asked passing strangers for directions, it seemed everyone in Little Rock knew about the woman, although nearly everyone told a different tale.

"Rumor has it, she murdered her father to take over his company. Then she seduced a half dozen honest businessmen to steal theirs!"

"She's a monster! I've heard wolves howling around that mansion of hers — seen strange things through the windows. Mark my words, she's not human!"

"All those stories are mere nonsense. She's just a powerful woman who knows her own mind. Some folk don't like that, is all."

The more Greta heard about the Snow Queen, the more uncertain she was about what the woman might want with Kit. It all seemed so fantastic, so unlikely. Then she considered the sleigh sitting covered by brush and branches on the outskirts of town. Unlikely and fantastic seemed to be her stock in trade this week.

By late morning, she'd made her way to the elegant town house located in a fashionable part of town.

Was Kit inside? Did she dare to just walk up to the front door and pull the bell?

As much as she longed to see his face again, to know he was alive and well, a part of her was also terrified. It could very well have been exactly as Captain Hamm suggested. Kit may have simply seized an opportunity. For all she knew, there was a telegram waiting back in St. Louis, explaining everything.

Or the Snow Queen could be a madwoman who was torturing him with alchemical poison while Greta fretted on the street corner.

"They've already left." A thin, reedy woman's voice reached her from a narrow alley running alongside the limestone mansion.

Greta looked into the windswept alley. She saw a plump old grey-haired woman in a black taffeta dress. A dark veil adorned her shabby black hat, which had once been fine.

"Who's already left?" said Greta warily.

"The young man and the Snow Queen."

"Who's to say I'm watching for anyone?"

"Your manner, girl. If you're not careful, you'll be run over by one of these infernal smoke-belching contraptions. You're not watching where you go, but you are watching for someone to come out of that house." She lowered her voice conspiratorially. "I know where you can find him. You follow a boy of about your age, of sturdy build, with dark hair and eyes? Have you come from Missouri?"

Greta's eyes narrowed. "How could you know that?"

The woman looked around as if concerned she was being watched. "Not here, my girl. Not in the open. If you care about the tinker, you must come with me this instant!"

❄ ❄ ❄

Greta hesitated. The woman looked harmless and genuinely afraid, clutching an enormous black leather satchel tightly to her chest, yet something seemed suspicious about her manner. Still, she clearly knew something about Kit. Regardless of whether Kit had come here willingly, simply marching up to the front door of the mansion and knocking didn't seem like the cleverest plan. An old woman's account had gotten her this far. How dangerous could it be to listen to this one?

Greta nodded, and followed her down an alley running the length of the town house.

The alley opened onto a winding, larger street. There were fewer people, and fewer conveyances compared to the bustling street she'd left behind. She followed a few paces behind the surprisingly spry woman. She halted in surprise as the older lady turned and headed towards the back of Evelyn DeWinter's property.

Attached to the back of the limestone mansion stood an immense steam garden conservatory. The building's copper and iron frame was streaked with green. Great panes of shimmering translucent glass stretched between the frames, at least two stories high. The woman pulled an ornate key from the folds of her dress, and unlocked the immense metal door. Greta followed her inside.

Inside, it was like a summer garden. Condensation dripped from pipes crisscrossing the enormous conservatory. Thick with vapor, the air hung with the rich scent of earth and growing things. Raised beds and the lush vegetation within them formed a verdant maze. The woman lead her to an enclosed room in the center.

To Greta's surprise, the room resembled a parlor. Two wing-backed chairs flanked a table set for tea. A worn Persian rug covered the polished wooden floor. Brick lower walls and a peaked tin roof created something like a gazebo or summerhouse. Fogged, dripping glass set in green-streaked copper frames formed the upper walls.

The woman in black settled into an armchair, laying the satchel in her lap, and gesturing to the other chair. "Please sit down. Here, we can speak freely. I'm quite certain we won't be heard. Evelyn and your young man left earlier this morning."

"How do you have a key? And how is this safer than talking in the street? What do you know about the young man I'm seeking? What's your part in all this?"

"One question at a time, my dear. I'm Isadora Halfacre. My husband was once employed by Evelyn DeWinter, and I still carry out small errands for her from time to time. That's how I have a key to the conservatory. With her gone, this is actually the safest place to talk. Her spies may scour the city streets, but they don't dare come in here. She's the one who took your young man." Mrs. Halfacre looked directly in Greta's eyes for the first time, which reassured her a bit.

"Took or hired? I just want to know if my friend is safe. He disappeared without a word, and that's not like him. I've heard a lot of rumors about this Snow Queen, and I'm not sure what to believe. People claim she's got more money than Midas, and a heart of ice."

"There is more truth to that last than you know," Mrs. Halfacre looked down. "She's capable of horrors you cannot imagine. That's why I knew I must help you. Perhaps you can stop her. For the love of God, someone must!"

"So she *did* take my friend?" Greta wasn't sure whether to be more worried or relieved. It was uncomfortably warm. She tugged at the collar of her dress, a trickle of sweat running down her temple.

"I assume he is a tinker or an engineer? Some sort of mechanic?"

"The best in the world," Greta said with absolute confidence.

"That makes sense." Mrs. Halfacre began pouring tea into two cups. She seemed out of breath. Greta supposed she must be parched from their brisk walk and the heat of the steam garden. "Evelyn herself is a brilliant alchemist, so she'd have no need of one. She's hired a succession of tinkers every few months for five years. None of them seem to know exactly what they're working on, but it's an enormous engine of some sort located in an airship near her largest coal mine in Pineville, in the republic of Kentucky."

"It can't be too big, if it fits in her airship."

"The one she brought from Missouri's just one of many she owns. The one currently anchored in Kentucky is a fortress four decks deep. It was my misfortune to be waiting at her townhouse when she arrived with your young man."

"Kit," Greta interrupted. "His name is Kit. And he's not my young man. He's a very dear friend."

"Then your friend is in terrible danger. The Snow Queen wants absolute power. It's all she's ever desired, as long as I've known her. As she's grown older, she's become obsessed with some form of the Philosopher's Stone. She's convinced she can succeed where the old alchemists failed. I overheard her speaking with one of her agents. Whatever her machine does, it will mean the end of thousands of people, perhaps millions!" She took a deep gulp of tea, and nudged the other cup towards Greta.

"Kit would never help anyone harm another soul, not willingly. What hold does she have over him?"

"I don't know," Mrs. Halfacre looked down at her teacup. "Of course, she can be quite persuasive to gentlemen, when she has reason to be. She's beautiful. And she can be charming, if she wishes. Perhaps she lied about what the machine will do. Many men have fallen prey to her deceit." A shadow of anger passed Mrs. Halfacre's face, but then faded to sadness.

"That's absurd!" Greta picked up the teacup and downed its contents in one swallow. "Kit's a master mechanic. Whatever the machine is, he'd recognize its purpose as soon as he saw it."

"Well, the people under her influence often fail to see things one would think were obvious. Don't underestimate her ability to manipulate others." Isadore looked searchingly into Greta's eyes.

"Don't be ridiculous." Greta leaned forward in her chair, and the room seemed to tilt at an odd angle. "Kit would never . . . would never. . . ." She paused in mid-sentence. The room whirled around her. "What? What have you done?" she muttered.

"I am so sorry, my girl." Mrs. Halfacre stood, and nudged Greta fully upright. The girl sat in perfect stillness, face glazed over, the alarm that had been etched across it replaced with a dull stare.

"As I said, Evelyn can be very persuasive. My life would've been forfeit if I'd refused to help her. My poor Hiram crossed her only once, and it was the last mistake he ever made. She's every bit as deadly as I've told you. That's why I cannot help you or your friend. You're both lost. You were, from the moment you crossed her path."

The woman fretted over the tea service, her nerves clearly frayed from the strain of maintaining her deceit, and the knowledge of its consequences. She picked up her satchel and grasped the girl's hand, leading her from the tea room through the garden to the door to the main townhouse.

"I'm supposed to leave you here for her butler to manage, but it's one of those 'gens. The moisture in here can't be good for it. Let's see if we can get you to the house, at least."

The two women moved slowly down the path. The drug slowed Greta, and Isadora was exhausted from the strain of pretense, age and the hot, languorous atmosphere of the steam garden. They passed through raised beds of roses, perfume hanging rich and heavy in the air. Tangled briars tumbled onto the brick paths between the beds. A thorny branch caught Greta's arm.

The sharp pain shook her slightly out of her stupor. What was that scent? She recognized it from somewhere. It had been a long time ago, but it seemed important. She struggled to remember what she had been doing only a moment ago. She needed to remember.

She stopped, digging in her heels. Isadora tugged on her arm, uncertain what was happening. Greta fought against the cloudy haze. She'd been doing something important. It had something to do with the flowers. Their perfume was so strong it was nauseating. A nameless fear boiled in her stomach. What were those flowers called again?

Red, with heavy velvet petals and thorns — roses!

They were roses. She loved roses. They were her favorite. She and Kit had planted roses in their garden. The important thing was close. She could almost see it. The old woman was whining something, dragging at her arm.

She remembered digging a small wooden box out of the dirt. Roses on the magnificent clockwork ring.

Kit. The ring.
Kit!

Greta blinked hard, doubled over and retched. Mrs. Halfacre had drugged her. She wrenched her hand free of the horrified woman's grip, scrambling backwards and turning to run. Halfacre lurched forward, trying to grab her before she escaped. Greta slipped out of her grasp, and the older woman fell into the disgusting mess on the brick path.

"No!" she screamed. "She'll kill me! I beg you, come back!" she sobbed from her knees, reaching out in desperation.

Greta patted the pockets of her pinafore frantically till she found a familiar flask. Pulling it out, she unscrewed the top and gulped a huge swig of the bezoar potion she always kept on hand. Many of the ingredients alchemists worked with could be poisonous. The potion countered most ill effects if taken quickly enough.

She reached the back door of the mansion, flinging it open in hopes that Kit's absence was another of Isadora Halfacre's lies. The chill air of the main house blasted her face, clearing the last traces of the drug from her mind.

A gleaming brass 'gen stood in the doorway blocking her path. She could see past it, straight down the long dark hall to the front door of the mansion.

Kit was walking out that front door. He was dressed in finer clothes than she'd ever seen him wearing, and he was facing away from her, but she'd recognize him anywhere.

"Kit!" she screamed, her voice hoarse. "Stop! I'm here!" She flung herself against the machine, but it was useless. The automaton wrapped its arms around her and squeezed, nearly crushing her. As her yell echoed down the long hallway, Kit glanced back and looked straight at her. He seemed puzzled. Someone called to him from the street below, and he turned and walked away.

"Nooo!" Greta felt all the air escape her lungs. Whether it was from the pressure of the 'gen's iron grip or the shock of seeing Kit leave, she couldn't tell. Tears burned her eyes. She could hear and smell Isadora Halfacre come up behind her.

She was trapped, and Kit had deserted her.

❄ ❄ ❄

"Please, let me go!" Greta screeched, wriggling in an attempt to free herself from the mechanical butler's brass arms. Isadora Halfacre skittered up behind her, reeking of vomit.

"Gaskon, I believe your mistress left instructions for what to do with the girl?" The relief in her voice was audible.

At the sound of Isadora's voice, Gaskon shifted, stiffening. Greta was convinced the machine was preparing to crush the life from her. She thrashed and kicked, screaming at the top of her lungs.

The 'gen's arms opened, but he maintained an iron grip on her wrist as she tumbled to the ground, flailing. Greta scrambled to her feet, struggling to pull her hand free. How could Kit just walk away and leave her in danger? Her chest ached, but she didn't know whether it was from the 'gen squeezing the breath out of her or from Kit ripping her heart out between her ribs.

A hollow voice echoed from the machine. "Isadora?"

Halfacre's eyes widened in strange recognition. The woman trembled, raising a hand to her lips. Greta froze at the eerie sound. No machine could create such a plaintive, human voice.

"Hiram?" The name Halfacre uttered was a whisper, breathed with the desperate wonder of a prayer.

"Where am I? What's happened to me?" The metallic voice sounded confused, bereft. Gaskon looked down at the jointed brass arms and hands, the elaborate scrollwork of engraving which etched out a uniform on the metal body. He lifted one leg, only to drop it heavily onto the floor where he stood, nearly cracking the polished marble tile.

"What has happened to me, Isadora?" The eerie, echoing voice vibrated with horror and rising panic.

Isadora Halfacre launched herself at the machine, wrapping her arms around it, tearing at the brass casings as if she could pry them away and find her lost husband beneath.

Greta watched in mute awe.

"Hiram! My God in heaven, is that really you? She told me you'd been killed. Crushed and buried in the factory! Dear God, are you really in that . . . that machine?" She turned to Greta, eyes mad with horror. "You! You're an alchemist, like *her*. You can fix this. Change him back! Do it, or I swear I'll . . . I'll have him pull your right arms out of their sockets!"

Greta felt her stomach lurch again. She had heard tales about such ancient, forbidden alchemy. Some claimed it was possible to take the spirit from a living creature and bind it to a mechanical construct. But surely ripping out a man's very soul would kill him?

"Please believe me. I'm an alchemist, but I'm nothing like anyone who'd do this. And no formulae I know of can change flesh into metal, much less change it back."

Halfacre gripped her shoulders, shaking her till her teeth rattled. "You have to do something! I swear, if you help me get my Hiram back, I'll help you find your young man. But you can't just leave us like this!"

She recalled the old woman in Riverside Park. Her description of the wolves which had chased Kit to the cliff had puzzled her. She couldn't imagine a machine he couldn't have easily outsmarted and outmaneuvered.

Now, the story she'd heard about wolves howling inside the mansion made sense. Could Evelyn's laboratory be somewhere in this townhouse?

"I think . . . I think I may be able to help."

The 'gen leveled its glass gaze at her. Isadora slumped against him.

"What can you do?" A shiver ran down Greta's spine at the spectral sound of his voice.

"I think I know how she did this. I'm not sure how she avoided the notice of the Alchemists Guild. They have measures which are supposed to notify them if anyone attempts this kind of experiment.

But I suspect the evidence will be in her laboratory."

"The basement." The words were a tinny growl.

"Can you show me?" Greta asked, trying hard not to let her voice squeak in fear. Isadora was still weeping, staring at her husband's bizarre and unfamiliar form with a mixture of disbelief, misery and hope.

"Follow me." The metal man released his grip at last. She wiggled her fingers as the blood rushed back to them.

Part of Greta wanted to bolt for the front door. A voice in her head told her every second took Kit further away. What use could she be to these poor souls? Still, she had to at least try and give them some peace. And there might be something here she could use to free Kit when she caught up to him again. It was becoming clearer with every moment that underestimating the Snow Queen could be a fatal mistake. As much as she wanted to rush after Kit, she realized now she might need more than her wits and a few incendiaries to save him.

Especially since it looked like he didn't *want* to be saved.

After several twists and turns down one hallway after another, Gaskon opened a door which revealed an iron stairwell spiraling down towards a lower level. Taking a deep breath, Greta slipped ahead of the other two and descended the stairs. She had no idea what horrors might await her, but she needed to know, as much as the Halfacres, what the Snow Queen had done.

Gaskon turned a dial, and, with a hiss, the gaslights in the chamber rose to illuminate the laboratory.

Greta gasped. It looked far too much like the laboratory she had destroyed only a day before. Tables were covered with all manner of beakers and glass tubes. Different apothecary jars were lined up in rows on shelves holding neatly labeled ingredients. The stone floor was marked with stains, deep gouges and burns.

Along one stone wall was a row of glass tanks filled with milky translucent fluid which glowed a pale green, dark shapes floating within each one. A tangle of copper pipes hung over them, with spiral wires extending down into the liquid. A blue-white spark sputtered at the corner nearest Greta.

In the brief bright glare, she shuddered as something moved within the tank. As much as she didn't want to look, she couldn't tear her eyes away. A tiny body was immersed in each tank.

Her horror grew as she realized the small forms were not quite human. Hands and feet which had only four digits swam in and out of view, along with facial features which were half-formed. She forced herself to continue surveying the room, her heart clenched with fear.

A surgical table was pushed off to one corner. As she approached it with trepidation, she noticed the cabinets lining two walls of the large room. Greta crept up slowly to the first cabinet, and brushed a layer of frost from the porthole window in the top.

Inside lay an enormous, shaggy wolf. As she peered into the porthole, it moved.

She shrieked and tumbled backwards onto the floor. Regaining her courage, she looked in the window again. The animal was just breathing. It was asleep. She examined the cabinet, quickly recognizing the iridescent glimmer of an alchemical seal.

"Mr. and Mrs. Halfacre! Come here, I think I've found something." Suddenly excited, she ran down the length of the room to the last cabinet.

That's how she'd got away with it.

They weren't dead, so the enchantment never alerted the Guild.

The creatures were in a deathlike sleep, their spirits miles away trapped in automata. She had no idea how to wake them, or what would happen if she tried. She brushed the layer of frost away from the glass on the final cabinet.

This time, she was not surprised to find a man's face inside.

He was an older gentleman, whose once-dark hair was streaked with grey. A clanking noise behind her told her the Halfacres had caught up.

"Is this him?" she asked Isadora. The woman knelt beside her, and peered into the window. A muffled sob escaped her. She nodded, too overcome with emotion for words.

Greta looked up at the gleaming brass and steel automaton. She couldn't imagine what kind of monster would think it acceptable to turn a living human into a machine. But she knew one thing for certain; she was getting Kit away from Evelyn DeWinter, whether he'd left willingly or not.

"Mr. Halfacre, your body appears unharmed. But the cabinet is protected by an alchemical seal. I'm not sure how to break it safely. Or what will happen if we do. It could break the binding that's keeping your soul where it is. It could set off an alarm that notifies the Snow Queen we're here. And even if it breaks the binding, I'm not sure what that will do to you."

Isadora seemed to recover her wits in the face of Greta's sober appraisal of the situation.

"Then do nothing, child. I cannot risk losing Hiram a second time. And if Evelyn finds out we've uncovered her secret, I can't imagine what she would do."

Greta bit her lip. Breaking open one of the cabinets could bring Evelyn, and Kit, rushing back to the town house. They could open one of the wolves' cabinets, to avoid the risk of killing Hiram Halfacre. Of course, rousing a maddened wild animal also seemed imprudent.

Based on the lack of recognition in Kit's face, he was under the influence of a powerful formulae. Isadora had mentioned the Snow Queen's network of spies and agents. They could easily find themselves outnumbered and outgunned, an even worse situation.

Their biggest advantage right now was letting Evelyn believe everything had gone according to plan. At least for the moment.

"I might know someone who can help. He works with the Alchemists Guild. If anyone can figure out how to get Mr. Halfacre back . . . where he belongs . . . safely, it's them. I assume they have an office here in Little Rock, but I *must* follow Kit." She handed Isadora the card Neal Simms had given her before she'd discovered Kit's disappearance.

Isadora nodded. "There's a telegraph machine upstairs in the parlor. I can wire them a message as soon as you leave. Oh! The message!" She opened the large handbag she'd been clutching and pulled a black metal bird from its depths, shoving it into Greta's hands.

"What is this?" A shimmer of alchemical enchantment flashed across the dull painted surface of the clockwork device.

"It's a messenger. She told me use it to tell her you were . . . that I'd. . . ." the elderly woman's voice broke.

"I know."

Greta gave Isadora Halfacre a look that spoke volumes. She squeezed the older woman's hand, and the older woman in turn nodded at the automaton which held the essence of the man she loved. Tragedy and terror drove people to awful things.

As each glance around the laboratory revealed more glimpses of Evelyn DeWinter's experiments, she shuddered to think what monsters the woman would make of ordinary people caught in her clutches for any length of time.

"She told me how to use the device. You press the wings against the body and speak your message. Then you press the wings again to make it fly to her to deliver it. Do you want me to send the message? Tell her you're . . . gone?"

Uncertainty slowly hardened into a flinty expression of resolve. "No."

Greta bolted for the stairs, more determined than ever to rescue Kit. She spared the Halfacres one last look as they clutched each other.

"I'm going to try to catch them before they leave the city. If I fail, I want her to know I'm coming."

CHAPTER 12
THE MAN IN THE MIRROR

Kit shivered in the ice palace, his breath escaping in ragged puffs. No matter how fast he ran, he could not catch up to the woman he pursued. Even when he slowed or stopped to rest, she did not leave him behind completely. He was left in a state of longing and confusion.

After running for what seemed like forever, he stumbled into a room filled with machine parts, all made of ice. The room looked less like a palace, and more like a warehouse hewn from slabs of ice. Unlike the rest of the labyrinthine structure, no elaborate scrollwork had been carved into the walls or support beams. The room's light flickered down from a plain-looking orb, unadorned except for the crystalline rivets which held the beams and slabs of ice in place.

He turned his attention to the jumble of machine parts lying scattered around the room. The gears looked like great snowflakes. He paused, overwhelmed by curiosity. Each piece had a single word etched on its surface in a fluid script, like a maker's mark.

"Eternity."

The word reverberated in his mind. A memory came tantalizingly close, tied to that word. He could almost see it, engraved inside a circle of polished metal. His head pounded with the effort to remember where he had seen it, but the harder he tried to recall it, the more agonizing the pain in his head became. He finally relented, and picked up one of the frozen gears. He could no longer hear the tapping of shoes ahead of him. Either the woman had disappeared or she was standing and waiting for him to pick up the chase again.

Was this his purpose? Had the woman been merely a guide to bring him to this room? Scanning the bits and pieces of machinery, he doubted it. These looked more like spare parts. The same way Michelangelo could see a finished sculpture in a piece of marble, he had the ability to see a completed machine in a pile of loose cogs.

He could remember nothing of his life before arriving in the palace. No warm memories of friends or family rose up to greet him, no matter how hard he tried to produce them. In fact, trying to do so resulted in a splitting headache, and a stabbing sensation in his chest.

Nevertheless, his head was far from empty. Plans, schematics, blueprints for all kinds of devices all floated in and out of his consciousness. He was a maker of some sort, but that was all he knew.

His reverie was broken by a woman's voice echoing through the halls.

"Find me, Kit. I need you."

The voice sounded familiar, but he couldn't quite place it. Discarding the frozen gears, he set off again in search of the elusive woman. There was only one door out of the room. As he ducked through it, he saw a flash of blue-green skirt swish around the corner.

The walls were translucent in this part of the palace. He could see her form, but the weird bending of light through the prismatic surface kept shifting her appearance. One moment her hair was white-blond. The next it was a honey-gold. Her dress similarly shifted hues and shapes. He had no idea who she was, but with all the certainty he possessed, he knew he must follow her.

He turned another corner, and pulled up short. A long empty hall stretched out before him, lined with mirrors. Each mirror's frame was carved in rich detail, and each one was different. Above him, light filtered down from sparkling chandeliers. A myriad of colors of light bounced around the room.

He strained his eyes, searching for the woman, but she was nowhere to be found.

A flash of blue in the mirror nearest him caught his eye. He looked into the reflection, and slipped backwards, startled. He looked down, to confirm he still wore the simple workman's attire he'd been dressed in all along. He scrambled to his feet and gazed into the glass again.

The man in the mirror moved in perfect synchronization with him. He was the right height, his hand looked the same when he turned it over in front of the reflection. But he was also very unlike him. Dressed in a tailored suit of rich grey fabric, the man in the mirror seemed confident and assured. A diamond stickpin held his silk cravat in place. Then the man smiled at him. There was a bit of a wicked gleam to that smile, which Kit found both fascinating and terrible.

Movement caught his eye in the corner of the looking glass. A woman in blue, with platinum hair slipped into the frame. She smiled at him through the mirror. It was a dazzling smile, but it held no warmth. The woman in the picture slipped her arm around his dapper reflection. Slowly, the background of the reflection came into focus.

The room the pair occupied was a luxurious parlor. Polished leather and wood surfaces gleamed, covered with the accoutrements of success.

The other Kit seemed to beckon to him.

"Join me. Become me."

Kit hesitated. The picture framed in the looking glass had its appeal, but there was something tugging at the edges of his mind which held him back. Brief flashes of another woman, very different from the elegant creature in the looking glass, surfaced in his mind. He stepped away from the mirror to look down the hall.

The other Kit looked back at him from all the reflections along one wall. The other wall showed a different view. He walked over to examine the other reflection. Like him, this Kit wore workman's clothing, except his were filthy and worn. He looked older than his years, exhausted by care. As this new reflection solidified, the background appeared to be a ramshackle workshop.

He waited for a moment, to see if the woman from the other side would join this version of himself. Or possibly the other woman he'd glimpsed for mere seconds in his mind's eye.

The other Kit shook his head.

"You failed. You lost her. She's gone."

The words echoed through his brain. This frame held but loneliness and failure.

He turned and crossed the hall, hand outstretched towards the surface of the other glass.

❄ ❄ ❄

Evelyn DeWinter sat placidly reading the papers in her traveling coach airship. The tinker slept on a chaise nearby, still under the influence of her formulae. He had seemed especially agitated for a moment as they left the town house, after pausing to look over his shoulder down the hall.

She had called to him from the steam carriage, bringing his attention back from whatever he thought he was leaving behind. The feeling you'd forgotten something was a common effect of the powder, but he obeyed too reluctantly, prompting another dose. He slipped into a drowsy stupor as soon as the Eurus had lifted off from the platform.

This particular craft was of middling size, not quite as fast as her day trip craft, but much smaller than the floating fortress they traveled towards. Pineville was an overnight journey even at full speed, and the traveling coach had been moored in Little Rock. It contained a comfortable bedchamber at the stern, the sitting room midship, and the bridge where Guthrie captained the ship at the bow.

She read The Gotham Gazette, a New York paper, which included an interview she had conducted a week before. In the interview, she alluded to an important announcement she'd be making soon concerning a technological advancement to alter the course of human history. She wasn't prone to hyperbole or exaggeration.

The reporter had sputtered in delighted curiosity at her bold pronouncement. It was, of course, entirely true. She simply omitted telling him not all of humanity would be delighted at the ensuing alteration. Nor did she mention many of them might not live to see the future.

She scorned the bourgeois governments of the new world, as much as the stiff royals of the old world, with their quibbling morality which objected to creating artificial life. It meant no one could know of her accomplishments, at least until her greatest experiment gave her the power to disregard them. She had the resources to buy a certain amount of freedom. She'd soon have the power to ensure total liberty to do as she pleased.

But first, she must complete the Eternity Engine. It had become her obsession since she first posited her theory. Soon, even Valentine would be forced to acknowledge the full extent of her genius. She would be the first alchemist to create an invention that offered the same effect as the philosopher's stone and the elixir of life. She had already created life, or at least transformed it, with her animatons. Why shouldn't she have the power of a god?

Of course, the journey had been fraught with danger and risk. What worthwhile adventure wasn't? Valentine had shown her the trick for getting around the Guild's notice when creating the animatons, but the blueprints for the Eternity Engine had been solely her design. Six months before, those plans had nearly been stolen. Some sneak thief had broken into her overseer's house in Pineville, and opened the safe which held an older copy of the plans.

Fortunately, the alchemical seals she'd placed on the safe and the house had released her prototype wolf and frightened away the burglar before he'd had a chance to take anything of consequence. The wolf animaton was supposed to eliminate the intruder and return. Evelyn had spent an anxious week, as

Gresham tracked the machine into the woods. The plans for the Eternity Engine, thankfully, had been left untouched.

Gresham returned to report that the machine had been destroyed. He found the battered shell of the machine propped up as a scarecrow in an old woman's garden. The crazy old bat had blown it apart with a shotgun blast. She claimed she saw it stalking through her property and fired on it, blowing the "infernal device" to "smithereens."

Evidently, she'd been quite proud of the feat.

More likely, there was a flaw in the machine's fabrication which caused the steam engine to overheat and explode. No mere shotgun shell could have done more than dent the thing's brass and steel hide. Her design of the later models had been more careful, all the same. The somnus formulae had kept the first wolf asleep in its cabinet even after the automaton was destroyed, and she'd been able to bind its animus to one of the new models.

Across the cabin of the Eurus, Merryweather groaned in his sleep. It required a stronger dose of the control powder than she'd anticipated to keep him entranced. She also needed to administer it more frequently than she'd expected. She'd encountered captains of industry whose wills were easier to bend than this simple mechanic's. Not that it mattered. Eventually, the powder would break his will, and the illusion of his infatuation with her would be the only reality which mattered to him.

A noise at the porthole attracted her attention. One of her mechanical ravens had landed on the edge, cocking its black tin head and cawing like a real bird.

It was the one she'd with Halfacre, along with instructions to notify her when the alchemist was unconscious. The tincture she'd put in the cup wouldn't kill the girl, just slow her heart to nearly a stop over the course of a few hours. She'd instructed Gaskon to bury the body, which would finish her off without triggering any alarms for the Alchemists Guild.

It was crucial the widow follow her instructions, and leave the girl's body in the conservatory for Gaskon to handle. After the automaton's strange pause, Evelyn had some concerns about the widow and the 'gen spending much time together. One trip to the basement laboratory, and things could unravel quickly.

The penalty was death for mixing alchemy and mechanics as she'd done to create her butler and her wolves. The evidence in her basement would call the full force of the Guild down on her, at the worst possible moment.

She grasped the bird, activating its recording. She expected to hear Halfacre, reporting her success. Instead, a young girl's voice rang out.

"I know what you are. I know what you have planned. And I'm coming to set Kit free."

The Snow Queen held her breath. A mere girl

couldn't have escaped her trap, much less captured and used her own clockwork raven. It was impossible!

The sound of the girl's voice carried across the parlor, and Kit moaned in his sleep. A troubled frown creased his face. He clutched his chest as if a warding off a stabbing sensation in his chest. After a few moments of writhing in pain without fully waking, he relaxed again into exhausted sleep.

Evelyn reached under her settee for the wooden case. She carried it into her cabin, locking the door behind her. She set the case on her mahogany dressing table, jerking it open and shoving the mechanical bird into it with the ferocity of a woman betrayed.

She took a deep breath, pulled out another raven, and set it on the dark wood. She pressed its black wings against its fragile tin form.

The raven cawed twice.

"The girl in this photograph follows me. She travels alone. Send evidence you've taken care of her."

The bird cawed twice more.

This raven's ring was held by Gregory, the Robber Baron of the Tennessee Caravan. They were always somewhere near Pineville this time of year. She pulled a newspaper clipping from the stack on her desk, a picture of Kit with the girl. She had underestimated their attachment, but it didn't matter.

She slipped the photo into an envelope, rolled it tightly and tied it to the bird's leg with a red ribbon. She picked up a tablet of alchemical coal from a box on her desk, dropping it into the bird's mouth.

She carried the raven back to the porthole, and said simply "Go."

It flew off behind them, bouncing in the late winter wind and eventually disappearing into the dark green shadows of the pines.

CHAPTER 13
THE ROBBER PRINCESS

Greta watched the ground approach. She busted the thin crust of ice in the bucket and poured water over the edges of the sleigh. She'd need to start a fire as soon as she landed; there was one last bottle of featherfall in her work box, but she'd have to activate it with a torch after applying it to the sleigh and reindeer. The Kentucky border had to be close by now.

She aimed for a clearing where the sleigh could land. She'd been flying exposed to the late winter wind for hours. Even though she'd practically buried herself in blankets, shawls and scarves, and Tennessee was a bit warmer than Missouri, she still felt miserable and half-frozen.

The sleigh landed with a thud, pine needles crunching beneath the locomotive tracks. Greta nearly fell over from the jarring impact. Once she'd rescued Kit, they would need to work on a better landing mechanism, perhaps something with coiled metal springs. A glass enclosure wouldn't be a bad idea, either.

She caught a flash of movement from the trees. Before she could reach into her work box for a weapon, colorfully dressed men and women ran out of the pine woods. They rushed towards her, yelling and whooping. She grabbed a wrench and raised it to fend off the robbers. The nearest man leapt onto the sleigh, her caught her wrist and twisted it, prying the wrench from her frozen fingers.

"Now, there, young 'un! There'll be none a that! Ain't no Yankee girl gonna get the jump on a member of the Caravan. Especially not when we been warned you were comin'!"

"Well, I'll be! Have a look at this here sledge. It's damn near all copper, yer Grace. We'll get a fortune for it, once we tear it down. The reindeer, too." A small, wiry man had hopped astride one of them. He patted its metal back as if stroking a living creature. His long, colorful knitted scarf blew in the wind, then got tangled in the reindeer's brass antlers.

"I dunno, Beau." said a grey haired man, stroking his grey beard as he approached. "We might get more for those reindeer if we leave 'em intact. Nice clockwork mechanics. Might be able to sell 'em to some feller who wants it to pull a cart. Might even trot 'em out at our own fairs for a bit, charge folks for a ride on 'em. We can always sell the copper once they break down."

The man who grabbed Greta's wrist had wrapped an arm around her waist and pulled her out of the sleigh. In a deft movement, he had both her arms pinned behind her, walking her over to the bearded man.

"Is she the one we're lookin for?"

The man gave her the same look of shrewd appraisal he'd given the reindeer and sleigh.

"I believe she is. I'll want to take her back to camp, look at 'er against the photograph her highness sent, just to be sure. Wouldn't do to slit this pretty thing's throat only to discover she's the wrong girl. We might get a handy ransom out of 'er alive."

The man chuckled and produced a rope from his belt. Greta was bound and gagged, carried over the shoulder of a very large vagabond into the darkening woods. Behind her, she could see a number of their band tearing Kit's sleigh to pieces.

"Bunch a potions in this box here, Gregory!" shouted the small man, Beau, who was looking into her workbox with a suspicious frown. "What d'ya want us to do with it?"

"Set it aside for now. Carefully! That stuff is prone to blowing a fella up, if yer not careful. I'll send Lulabelle out in the mornin to look through it and see what we can salvage. Just leave it near the reindeer for now."

It seemed to Greta as if they would be bouncing through the brambles forever. Branches reached out and scraped across her arms, legs and face. She grunted the few times the man carrying her stumbled in the dark, his shoulder jamming into her empty stomach.

Finally, they came out of the woods into a clearing lit by a huge bonfire. Painted wagons and silk tents circled the clearing. Felled trees made benches all around the fire, and a village of men, women and children filled the space. Some of them played traditional songs on banjos, fiddles and flutes, while others danced. Some were eating, and a small group encircled a young man who was telling an animated story, prompting uproarious laughter.

The man carried her to the largest wagon, a bright red one festooned with gilt decorations. He opened the door at the back of the wagon, and tossed her to the floor inside, calling up to the wagon's single occupant, a young woman no older than Greta.

"Lulabelle! Yer father's asked I drop this bit a' baggage here for the night. Don't get attached to 'er. She's most likely the one 'er Highness wants dead. Yer pa just wants to check the picture again in the mornin to be sure. She's got a box of chemicals out near the road. Yer to look into what we can take safely in the mornin."

The girl nodded and waved him away. "I got 'er, Joseph. You go on now. Getcha a bite to eat."

The man nodded and shut the wagon door. It made a peculiar room. Two hammocks with blankets swung from the roof. A small, rough desk sat at the opposite end. A heavy chest sat in a corner. The girl Lulabelle leaned back on a three legged stool before a dressing table, turning around to look at Greta, who had never seen such a wild-looking young woman.

Instead of a proper dress, she wore buckskin breeches tucked into dark leather boots which came nearly to her knees. A velveteen corset with an oriental pattern held her billowy muslin tunic in place. Her thick brown leather belt held a small holstered revolver on one side, and a wicked sheathed blade at the other. A patterned scarf kept riotous red hair away from her face, while gold hoops hung from her ears.

The girl's pale skin had so many freckles it was nearly tan, and her eyes were such a dark brown they were nearly black. Despite her delicate features, she looked like a wild animal escaped from the circus.

Greta began squirming, attempting to talk through the gag in her mouth.

A wry grin crossed Lulabelle's face.

"I ain't sure what'd be funnier. Listenin to you try to talk through that thing, or hearin whatever tall tale you spin tryin to save yer hide." She unsheathed her knife and cut the gag away. "Well, it ain't like I can't just gag ya again later, if I get tard of yer yappin. So what d'ya have to say fer yerself?"

Greta held her tongue. First, because the gag had made her jaws tired, and second, because she knew she had one chance to convince this woman to let her go. It seemed a slim chance, given how cavalier the girl had been at her captor's pronouncement that her father intended to kill Greta first thing in the morning.

"Do you get stuck guarding a lot of murder victims for your father?" she snapped.

The girl threw back her head and laughed, slapping her knee. "A few," she said. "None who ever asked fer a head count, though. That's a first!"

"Well, I can guarantee none of them had as good a story as mine." Greta had an idea.

"Well, do tell! I love a good yarn." The girl leaned back against the desk, folding her arms in front of her and kicking her boots out as if settling in.

"My name's Greta Singleton. I'm an alchemist from St. Louis in the republic of Missouri."

"I know where St. Louis is. I'm not a fool."

"Didn't say you were. Are you going to let me tell my tale or not?"

"My apologies, Madam Sheherazade," said the girl with a wink. "Please do continue."

"Since I was five, I've lived next door to the best friend any girl could have. I've singed his arm hair off, gotten him in trouble with the police, and blown up more of his possessions than I can even count thanks to my crazy experiments.

"Two days ago, he watched me blow up my parents' garden shed. If he hadn't pulled me back, it might have carried me into the sky with it. I'm not certain how he's managed to survive being my friend all these years, much less why he's continued to want my friendship—"

"How'd yer garden shed end up airborn?" Lulabelle interrupted with obvious skepticism. Even to her own ears it sounded like a tall tale, but the girl looked curious to hear the rest.

"I was trying to create an anti-gravity formulae. Something to make solid objects float like balloons. It worked. Really well. Too well."

"Is that how you made yer sled contraption fly? One of our scouts spotted ya in it a few miles back, came back on horseback to report to Pa. Said he'd never seen such a thing. They were gonna try to lasso ya and pull ya down if ya hadn't landed anyway."

"Yes," said Greta. "Kit, my friend, made the sleigh for a Christmas exposition. The reindeer can move with clockworks, and it had locomotive tracks and a tiny steam engine. His design was better than any of the horseless carriages I've seen. He's the best tinker in the world. He'll be a great engineer someday, if he survives whatever the Snow Queen has planned. If *any* of us survive what the Snow Queen has planned."

Lulabelle raised a suspicious eyebrow at the last ominous sentence.

"I suppose this is where ya try to convince me I have to let you go," she said drily.

"Does that mean you want me to skip past the part where I found out Evelyn DeWinter kidnapped my best friend, or the part where she hired a woman to drug me in Arkansas, and most likely kill me later? You want me to skip telling you she's planning on using Kit to build some sort of doomsday device that will probably be the death of all of us?"

"We'll be all right," said Lulabelle with a curt nod. "People have been tryin to kill the Caravan for a hundred years, and they tried to get rid of our people back in the old world fer even longer. We're survivors. Whatever Her High and Mighty the Snow Queen has planned, we'll do just fine. Don't you worry 'bout that, none. You best worry about your own self."

There was a smug tone behind Lulabelle's words, but also a tiny bit of something else. Bravado? Uncertainty?

"Maybe you're right, Lulabelle. I don't know much about the Caravan. You certainly seem like a capable group. But I'm also guessing that if the Snow Queen says jump, your father asks 'How high?' From what I've seen the last two days, everyone on earth who has a passing acquaintance with Evelyn DeWinter is terrified of her. She's a murderous witch, and I think you know she's capable of anything, including something your Caravan doesn't expect and just might not be prepared to handle."

"That may be true," said Lulabelle, looking at Greta from under half-lowered eyelids. "But we know what she'll do if we don't do what she asks. I'm not puttin my Pa, nor any of my kin, in a pine box to save your sorry hide!"

Greta started to retort back, but then shut her mouth. It was no use. She and her own father weren't close, but she loved him and believed he loved her, despite his constant complaints about her behavior. She'd never do anything that would lead to his death. She could do nothing to convince Lulabelle to sign her own father's execution order.

She began to cry. Greta did not cry often, and here she was, crying for the third time in two days. Then again, it had been an especially trying two days.

She'd failed. She couldn't rescue Kit. She couldn't even rescue herself. In the morning, Lulabelle's father would probably pull a knife — just like the one his daughter carried — across her throat, and that would be the end of Greta Jane Singleton. If not for the small matter of her being the only person who might be able to stop the Snow Queen from bringing about some sort of pernicious doomsday, the world would probably be a better place.

She would never see Kit again. The trickling tears became a full-blown sob. She wept as she had when she found his tattered coat by the edge of the Mississippi. She slid down the wall until she lay in a crumpled ball on the floor of the wagon.

"Now, there, don't be bawlin girl. I'm sorry, but it ain't no use. We all gotta die sometime. your time is just comin a little earlier than you mighta planned."

Good grief, thought Greta through her sobs. If this was Lulabelle's idea of comfort, thank God she probably had few occasions to try and console someone.

"I'm *hiccup* not *hic* crying because I'm going to die," said Greta miserably. "I'm crying because . . . because. . . ."

She began wailing. It was an awful sound. So awful Lulabelle seemed to consider stuffing the gag back in her mouth. But since that would probably choke her to death in her current state, in the end she must have decided it'd be best to just calm her down.

"Shh! It'll be all right. Now settle down, girl! You'll have my Pa in here in a minute, and he'll have both our skins — mine for takin the gag off in the first place, and yours for being purely exasperatin!" She leaned down and tried to stroke Greta's back.

Greta stopped wailing after a minute. She felt almost numb.

"So if you're not grievin leavin the mortal coil, what's ailin ya?"

Greta shifted backwards, working herself up into a seated position. "Reach into the pocket of my pinafore. You'll find a small wooden box. Please take it out. You want to know why I'm upset? I'll do more than tell you. I'll show you."

Her voice sounded resigned. She was done fighting the inevitable. She was done fighting her own heart. She would die before she ever got the chance to tell Kit the truth. She might as well tell someone.

Lulabelle reached into her pocket and pulled out the wooden box. She opened it, and stared at the expertly-crafted ring. "I've seen a lotta rings in my time. We pull 'em off travelers first thing, and I don't mind tellin ya, I ain't never seen a thing like this before."

She held it up to the lantern light. She examined the beautiful carving, and noted the inscription, but then she frowned as she turned it in her rough hands. "Hmm . . . what's this?"

"What's what?" Greta sniffled.

"Whenever we commandeer a wagon or carriage, Pa always sends me in to check for hidden trap doors and secret compartments. Got a bit of a sixth sense for secrets, and right now, it's tellin me this here ring's got one." With a practiced touch from years of picking locks, she grasped it with the thumb and forefinger of both hands, pulled apart, and twisted.

A soft tune played like a tiny phonograph. Even with Lulabelle's kinfolk singing and yelling outside, the two young women could still make out the sound.

"Well ain't that a kick in the pants. This might be the most amazing thing I ever seen."

She looked down to see Greta quietly crying again.

"It's Gilbert & Sullivan," she whispered. "My favorite song. He made it for me. He tried to give it to me, the day she took him. He tried to ask me to marry him, and I thought he was there to tell me he was leaving to take a job somewhere else. I slammed the door in his face.

"I've nearly killed both of us, I never listen, and I look like a hurricane blew me in most days. I'd make an awful wife. I probably shouldn't be trusted near small children. But he made that for me, and he wanted to ask me to marry him."

"What about you?" said Lulabelle "Do you love him?"

Greta locked eyes with the robber maiden, and said "More than life. So much I couldn't ever let myself admit it, because I couldn't imagine he felt the same. So much I was going to try to talk him out of marrying me, because I thought he'd be happier with someone else. Someone more normal, I suppose. He deserves a normal life. One without exploding, levitating garden sheds."

"Girl, I have never met this man a' yours," said Lulabelle, holding the ring in one hand and peering through the center of it at her. "Probably never will. But I can tell ya this. No man who'd make a ring like this, for someone like you, would ever be satisfied with somebody *normal*."

An outcry raised just outside the wagon. The door burst open, and the grey haired Robber Baron flung a bound and beaten man into the wagon next to Greta. His greasy dark hair was slicked back away from sharp-edged features, and he was nearly swallowed by a charcoal grey greatcoat.

"Our men found *this* skulkin outside camp. There's a telegram in his pocket from Her Highness, tellin him to kill me and set fire to the camp once he makes sure the girl is dead. That dirty double-crossin witch was plannin to do me in no matter what I do!" he shouted. "And I gotta tell ya, it don't make me too terribly inclined to comply with her requests!"

CHAPTER 14
COLD HEARTED

The Boreas, if not the largest airship on earth, was still quite large enough for Kit to find awe-inspiring. As the lift platform swayed beneath his feet, he gaped up at the lines and angles of the massive craft. Like everything which surrounded Evelyn DeWinter, it was luxurious, beautiful, intimidating and remote.

He gripped the case containing the plans for the engine she'd requested he work on. It hadn't taken much more than a cursory look for him to apprehend what she had been trying to build. The designs outlined an engine to halt or even reverse the aging process, indefinitely. Instead of trying to formulate the philosopher's stone in a laboratory, she had built a machine to achieve the same effect.

But it was more than that. The plans and schematics, along with the notes, made it clear the engine was a complete amalgamation of engineering and alchemy. It was difficult to say exactly where one science ended and the other began. The drawings were infinitely complex and the notations were almost inscrutable.

Yet he'd understood them easily. While he knew he was no alchemist, it was clear he'd somehow acquired much more than a passing knowledge of the arcane science. Unfortunately, attempting to remember how he'd come by the knowledge resulted in another splitting headache and a feeling of intense dread. The strange, melodramatic reaction seemed at odds with the pragmatic mechanical man he appeared to be in all other respects. It was peculiar to be such a mystery to himself. But if he had to injure himself, he was grateful to have fallen into the hands of the lovely Miss DeWinter.

As the bow of the great airship loomed closer, he wondered how he could possibly find his sleeping berth in such a flying behemoth. His sleep had been restless since the day he'd awakened on the Aeolus. Perhaps Miss DeWinter had been correct, and he'd struck his head while escaping the mechanical wolves. It would account for the troubled sleep, and the more troubling issue of his lost memories. It was fortunate she'd been seeking his services as a mechanic at the time. He was thankful she hadn't decided to employ someone else. She insisted his reputation as a tinker made him invaluable. He only wished he could remember earning that reputation.

Perhaps it didn't matter who he'd been before. What could he have known in his previous life which could have compared to being near her? Still, the nightmares grew steadily worse, even physically painful. They were always the same. He was trapped in a palace of ice, running towards something which seemed of paramount importance.

He had no more time to consider his dreams, as the lift platform slipped into a rectangular bay opening in the bottom of the Boreas. His eyes adjusted to the comparatively dim light indoors, and he could survey the spacious cargo bay. Crates and barrels, boxes and stacks of supplies all made neat rows and hallways around him. A 'gen painted with the livery of the DeWinter family stood at the edge of the open bay. It threw a large iron switch, turning off the chugging steam winch. The chains creaked as the platform slowed to a stop.

"Master Merryweather. Please follow me to the mistress." The 'gen turned and walked towards a set of doors several yards away. The rote pings of his mechanical voice were jarring. He'd grown accustomed to Gaskon, Evelyn's townhouse butler, who spoke much more naturally.

Kit followed the 'gen through a twisting maze of corridors and up stairs until he rapped on a door. A brass plate hung from it, inscribed with the words "Governor's Suite." Glancing down the corridor, he noticed similar plates on all the doors. Evelyn had purchased a luxury liner airship for personal use.

Extraordinary!

"Come in, please." The sharp notes of her voice pierced the wooden door, and Kit entered. The 'gen shut the door behind him.

"Good morning, Miss DeWinter." Kit smiled at the vision before him. She was bathed in light pouring in through four porthole windows. A dress of shimmering blue and white swirled around her as she moved, and her white blond hair coiled in elaborate twists and curls at the back of her head.

This was clearly the suite's parlor. Evelyn gestured to a chair covered in rich indigo velvet.

"Good morning, Kit. Have a seat. Have you made any sense of the schematics?"

He sank into the plush cushion. "Yes, Miss. I think I have a good grasp of the problem."

"Problem?"

"Well, in looking at these plans, there's clearly a flaw which would prevent it from working."

At this, her pale eyebrows rose to nearly her hairline.

"In fact, there's a series of — well, flaws may not be the correct word. It's almost as if some of the mechanical elements have been deliberately designed to fail."

Kit could have sworn the temperature in the room dropped twenty degrees. A look of cold hatred passed over his hostess, but she recomposed herself quickly.

"I see. It seems some of your predecessors took exception to my success. Tell me, Kit, can you correct these design flaws?"

"Certainly."

"And how long do you think it will be before we can test the engine?"

Kit frowned. Mechanical work was always difficult to judge, even with accurate plans. Tasks that should only take a few minutes could draw out into hours if the right tool or material wasn't on hand. He decided a conservative estimate would be the best choice. "I think I can have the machine operational in perhaps a day, maybe two. Certainly no more than a week, depending on parts and materials."

For the first time since he'd met her, the Snow Queen seemed to relax. "Are you quite sure? That is a much shorter timeline than my last engineer provided."

"With all due respect, Miss DeWinter, from what I've seen of those plans, your previous engineer may have been taking you for a buggy ride. Perhaps he or she needed the additional money a longer project would provide?"

Evelyn considered this for a moment, her eyes narrowed, and an odd smile playing at the corners of her mouth. "Perhaps. In that case, they've received their just payment. And now, thanks to you, my engine can finally be completed."

"My pleasure, ma'am."

At this, she gave him a look of dismissal. "This is very good news, on the whole, Kit. Please go get settled in your stateroom. When you're ready to begin work, any of the 'gens aboard can take you to the engine."

Disappointed in her sudden loss of interest, Kit turned and headed out the door, following the 'gen who had brought him up. He hoped she would be impressed enough by his ability to assess the problem to take a more personal interest in him.

Frowning a bit, he decided his best course of action was to complete the engine as quickly as possible. If he proved himself as skilled as he claimed to be, perhaps then she would take the kind of notice of him he deserved.

❄ ❄ ❄

The rap at the door was unexpected and unwelcome. The tinker could not have completed the Eternity Engine yet, and Evelyn was not anxious to speak to anyone else until it was finished.

"I'm not to be disturbed!" Her voice cut sharply through the polished wood of the stateroom door.

A low chuckle preceded the response. "You are already disturbed, according to most reports."

Ice water slid through Evelyn's veins at the sound of Valentine's voice. No! It was too soon. She intended to wire him as soon as the Eternity Engine had completed its first successful test.

When she had been transformed into an immortal, with thousands dead in sacrifice, he'd be forced to show her the respect she deserved. He'd realize she was more than his equal. Through Valentine, she would get the acknowledgment she'd never received from her father.

She was very close. Closer than she'd ever been. At this point, with Kit working on the engine as they spoke, there was nothing anyone could do to stop her.

Perhaps this was for the best. She never knew where on earth Valentine might be. What if, in some horrid coincidence, he'd been in the range of the cold wave? Then she would never hear his words of shocked respect, never get to see those perennially narrowed eyes widen in awe at her accomplishment.

She carefully adjusted her tone. "Valentine! This is a pleasant surprise. You so rarely make a personal appearance." She glided to the stateroom door and opened it. "I'm afraid you've caught me unprepared to properly entertain visitors, at least in this room. Come, let's repair to the observation deck. I can't offer you much in the way of luxuries, but I can offer a rather spectacular view of the mountains."

"If you say so, Evelyn. I don't think this visit will take long." She guarded her features against the frown threatening to appear at that statement.

"Once you hear how my plans have been proceeding, you may change your mind, my friend. You might wish to extend your visit a few days to see this particular experiment first hand." She graced him with a dazzling smile.

It took only a few minutes to traverse the winding passageways from her stateroom to the observation deck. It was an immense room, intended to serve as a ballroom in the Boreas' original purpose as a luxury cruise ship.

The front wall was filled with banks of windows glittering in the early morning light. Clouds drifted past, shimmering white like drifts of fresh snow. The sight never failed to entrance Evelyn. It was so clean up here. So perfect. Unmarred by the dirty, scrabbling messes people tended to leave in their wake.

Once the Eternity Engine was complete, the ground below would be like this, scourged clean and white with snow.

Valentine cleared his throat. He picked up a glass of sherry offered by one of her 'gens. "I was most displeased with your lack of progress on our project, my dear. I believe I was clear in my last message. Imagine my distress when I learned that instead of remaining in Little Rock to move things along, you'd flown halfway across the country to Appalachia. One might be tempted to think you've given up."

"Valentine, you must see reason. I've attempted every experiment you've asked of me. The homunculi are a dead end. But here, I've found a better means to the same objective."

"I doubt that very much, my dear. For one thing, I don't think you fully understand my goals." The man's sharp black brows folded inward and his lips made a thin line beneath his narrow black mustache.

"You want power. You want immortality. This ship holds the key to both!"

At this, Valentine burst into laughter. "You silly woman. You mean your ridiculous Eternity Engine? Why should I want immortality, when I already possess it?"

Evelyn's eyes widened in shock.

How could he possibly know?

"What do you mean?" A chill passed over Evelyn as a certainty she refused to acknowledge settled in her mind.

"I've had the formulae for the philosopher's stone for quite some time. What, do you think someone comes by this much knowledge in a single lifetime? I've known about your machine for months. I must say, it's certainly a novel approach. Not a particularly simple or elegant solution compared to the dozens who've come before you. But most definitely a novel one."

"You lie!" she hissed. It couldn't be. The philosopher's stone was the mystery of the ages. It had waited for her to unravel its secrets.

Another amused chuckle erupted from the dark haired imp of a man. "Oh, Evelyn, I wish you could see your face right now. You really should school your expression a bit better. You'll get wrinkles frowning so."

Evelyn recomposed herself. "Perhaps you do tell the truth. Maybe others have solved the stone. But the engine does more than grant immortality.

You want an army? With this ship, I can conquer nations without setting foot on the ground. Complete subjugation, without bloodshed."

Valentine raised an eyebrow, sneering at her. "You think because you can freeze men where they stand, your hands will be clean? You are far too literal. And you still fail to comprehend what I mean to accomplish. I have no interest in your flying icebox, even if you can get it to work."

Evelyn stood near the bank of windows, crestfallen. In Valentine she'd seen an equal creature, a man who could appreciate her talents and strength of will without moral judgment. It was a foolish sentiment. She would be better off without him. Without the illusion that anyone was her equal. Let him leave. Let that smarmy smile freeze solid on his face.

She needed no one.

"My dear Evelyn, it's become clear our association has reached an impasse. It's a pity. You did have such potential. I'll be taking my leave. I'll also be taking the tanks from your laboratory."

Evelyn smothered a smile. "Certainly. I have no use for them, and I very much doubt they'll ever amount to more than a peculiar set of disgusting dolls." If Kit completed his work as quickly as he'd promised, her erstwhile partner would be dead long before he could reach them. "My servants will see you out."

With that, Valentine flashed a wicked smile.

"Oh, that won't be necessary, my dear. I'll see myself out."

And with that, he whirled on his heel. A flash of smoke and light exploded at his feet, and in an instant he'd disappeared entirely.

CHAPTER 15
ALLIES AND ALCHEMY

It was early morning. Greta found herself outfitted like a member of the Caravan, standing in the same clearing where her sleigh had been dismantled. She couldn't decide if her odds of surviving, much less saving Kit, were better or worse than they'd been last night.

Lulabelle's father, the Robber Baron of the Caravan, had agreed to let her go. But she was under strict orders to find Evelyn DeWinter and either kill her or bring her back as a hostage. As part of the agreement, she had to be ceremonially "mustered in" as a member.

The ceremony had taken place in front of the roaring bonfire in the middle of camp last night. Gregory had cut her hand with a wicked-looking knife. Lulabelle had volunteered to have her own hand cut. The two young women had clasped hands over a flaming torch, and Greta had to repeat a vow of loyalty.

At the end, the crowd erupted into loud whoops and songs, and Lulabelle had bandaged their hands with some clean muslin. The musicians struck up a lively tune, and Greta had been obliged to dance with nearly every man, woman and child in the camp. A wiry older woman had offered her a flask, insisting it would take the sting out of her hand.

A sip from the flask had definitely taken her mind off the cut on her hand. It felt as though it seared the skin from her throat and burned away most of her nose hairs, as well. She'd gagged, coughed and sputtered, but the woman only laughed. It seemed like the revelry would last all night, but eventually she'd been allowed to tumble into Lulabelle's caravan and fall asleep on a pile of cushions.

She'd been awakened at dawn and dressed in some of Lulabelle's cast off clothes. Buckskin breeches and tall leather boots replaced her heavy wool skirts and high-button shoes. A flowing yellow blouse replaced her buttoned-up wool bodice. She wore a deep red corset over the blouse. It was a little uncomfortable, but Lulabelle insisted the steel boning had saved her life on more than one occasion.

A scrawny young man had lent her a long duster coat, as well as a belt with a sheath and holster. She'd bound her hair back into its usual braids, wrapped around her head and pinned tightly in place. She felt quite dashing in her new attire.

As soon as she was dressed, she had promptly been dragged back to the clearing to plan her daring mission of rescue and revenge. She had to hand it to them. Once the Caravan decided upon a course of action, they certainly didn't waste any time.

If she hadn't just agreed to go on a suicide mission where failure meant the end of the world, it all would have been quite exhilarating.

The sleigh was a complete loss. They'd reduced it to a neat stack of brass and copper plates faster than Greta would have believed possible. But the reindeer were still intact, and she still had her last bottle of featherfall and her alchemical work box.

She knew she could get one of the reindeer aloft with the featherfall formulae. She just needed to figure out a way to propel it, preferably at a high rate of speed. Sails? Something like a kite? The reindeer lacked a steam engine, and its clockworks weren't powerful enough to run the propeller fans she'd mounted to the sleigh.

Lulabelle came wandering up behind Shep, the scrawny young man who'd provided Greta with a coat and belt. He'd offered her his jaunty top hat, but she'd declined. Flying into a stiff wind didn't bode well for fine haberdashery.

"If only I had some of those Chinese rockets," she muttered, rummaging through her box of compounds for something useful.

"Did you say you needed some rockets? Like firecrackers?" Lulabelle asked.

"Yes," she said, "But I'd hardly expect to find

KATINA FRENCH

something so exotic in the middle of Tennessee, no offense."

"We run down a wagon train full of Chinese fellers just last week!" Shep exclaimed.

"They was on their way east from San Francisco. I reckon we have a whole box a' them rockets," added Lulabelle. "But you gotta have a flame to light 'em with."

Greta did some quick thinking. She always had at least a box of matches with her. She might be able to treat the rockets with a formulae to make them burn slower, while boosting their energy to propel the reindeer through the air.

"Can you go get me those rockets please, Shep?" she asked, as sweetly as she could manage. When he left, she ran over to the pile of debris that had once been Kit's sleigh. She looked at the crate of Christmas decorations she brought along, thinking she might be able to use their raw material to fashion something helpful.

The Snow Queen was using illegal alchemy to steal the souls of living creatures and make mechanical servants that possessed a mind, but were robbed of conscience or will. For years, Greta felt guilty for the accidental consequences of her experiments, but she'd always obeyed the law, never dabbling in any darker experiments.

Perhaps she could make a machine that could truly think for itself. Or at least, one that could react in a logical way. She and Kit had been thinking about turning the angels into something to ward off burglars. Could that idea really work?

She picked up a brass angel, running a finger over its sharp metal wings and looking at the spiky metal harp it held in its hand. The angels held a series of tiny metal drums, punched with instructions to fly, to sing, and to play their harps on command. If she could adjust the actions they performed, and use a formulae link and trigger the individual actions into something like a chain reaction, they could be used for defense.

She wouldn't create lifeless-yet-immortal creatures like Evelyn had done with Hiram Halfacre and the wolves. She wasn't going to try to play God.

She just prayed He'd grant her the skill to recruit a little divine intervention.

CHAPTER 16
THE END OF ETERNITY

The Snow Queen stood before a great picture window on her massive airship. Standing at the front of the observation deck, she enjoyed the feeling of the world at her feet. Her pale blue brocade gown, with a white watered silk underskirt swished across the parquet floor. A diamond necklace with a snowflake pattern glittered on her neck, and sparkling diamond snowflakes dangled from her earlobes.

She was nearly forty. While still ravishingly beautiful, she knew she had been even more so at twenty.

She would not fade quietly, growing old and bowed by time. Her power and beauty were her birthright. No matter what Valentine said, no one else had the courage, the brilliance, or the bold determination to pursue alchemy and engineering to their logical end. Let others accept limitations imposed by fools and cowards. She knew she had none.

The tinker was even better than she'd hoped.

He'd settled into his stateroom and immediately set to work on the Eternity Engine. After only a few hours, he understood completely what she had set out to achieve, even exposing the betrayal of her previous engineers.

He'd drawn a fresh set of blueprints by hand, tracing over the previous work, and adding in his own more elegant solutions. Her other engineers had been working on parts of the machine. This young man not only knew how to put those pieces together and calibrate them, he knew how to improve each piece to work even better. He had just sent word with one of her 'gens that the Engine was finally ready to be tested.

His experiences with the girl in Missouri had given him an excellent theoretical understanding of alchemy. Now that the girl was dead, he wouldn't be distracted in the midst of his work.

Thinking about the girl reminded her of the ravens she'd sent out. Gresham's should have returned to her by now. She had sent him to clean up whatever mess was left behind in Tennessee. The girl should be dead, the Robber Baron dispatched and his vagabond clan in disarray. Perhaps he'd encountered some difficulty.

She lifted her opera glasses, scanning the sky as she pondered what kept her agent from sending word, when she saw the answer careening into view.

A shiny copper reindeer flew towards the

airship. Its legs kicked as if running through the air. Some device bolted to its metal belly, the size of a small barrel, belched out a tail of flames and colored sparks. Sitting astride it, a girl with caramel-colored braids, wearing a pair of goggles, leaned over its neck as it blasted forward, her long coat whipping in the wind. Even dressed in the outlandish clothing of Caravan folk, it could only be the girl from the newspaper clippings — Kit's young alchemist friend.

Why was she not dead?!

The answer was clear. Gresham had failed her, and Gregory had betrayed her.

Evelyn whirled, storming across the observation deck to a gilded chest. Men might be unreliable as the weather, but devices at least always worked according to design. Inside the chest lay twenty gleaming silver snowflakes, their edges honed razor sharp. She lifted one carefully between both hands, and twisted her palms, releasing it. It whirled in the air like a maple seed, bobbing up and down.

In short order, she had activated them all. They hovered before her, awaiting instructions. A flock of bluebirds had been a small price to pay for such agile, deadly weapons.

She strode to the windows, flung one open and pointed at the girl.

"Kill her! Don't stop until she is dead, and once she is, fly into the nearest river and remain until you disintegrate!"

The snowflakes obeyed, buzzing out of the window towards the girl on her clockwork reindeer like a swarm of gleaming bees.

❄ ❄ ❄

Greta saw several objects fly out of the massive gondola of the ship. She reached into the saddlebags thrown over the reindeer, and began pulling out the angels. "Protect me and the reindeer," she croaked through the blasting wind. Their wings buzzed like hummingbirds. Each one flew off towards the snowflakes.

❄ ❄ ❄

The silver snowflakes hovered and spun, darting in towards her whenever an opening appeared in the phalanx of angels. Gripping the reindeer with one arm, Greta yanked out the Caravan blade from its sheath and smacked away a snowflake as it buzzed dangerously close. Another one glanced off the rump of the reindeer. She shifted her weight back and forth, hoping to use the reindeer's antlers as a shield against the relentless attack. Chiming notes of Christmas carols added to the noise of battle. She had forgotten to disable the music boxes within the angels when she'd modified them.

Sparks flew as brass clashed against silver. The sun glinted in dazzling reflections off the shiny, whirling combatants. A snowflake clipped Greta's arm before an angel drove it off, battering it with its harp.

She dove with the reindeer beneath the airship, holding on tightly as the reindeer barrel-rolled. One of her incendiary devices slipped out of the saddlebag. It fell to the ground, followed by an enormous explosion.

* * *

Evelyn smiled with satisfaction. She ran to the side of the ship, scanning the ground. A small crater marked where the girl and her monstrosity of a flying machine incinerated themselves.

At last. She turned from the window. She'd celebrate with a glass of champagne, and then finally, she would use the Engine. Nothing and no one stood in her way any longer.

* * *

Beneath the gondola of the airship, Greta still spiraled and twisted on the reindeer, while the angels dispatched the silver snowflakes. When two angels relentlessly beat the last one into crumpled junk, she spotted an open bay at the back of the bottom deck.

She aimed the reindeer at the opening. Before she flew through it, she pulled a cord to douse the rockets. The reindeer skidded across the deck, Greta rolling off it as it went. It was not the most elegant landing, but any landing you could walk away from was a good one, especially when one was flying a jet-propelled Christmas decoration.

Fortunately, the Snow Queen's need for secrecy had led to a skeleton crew, and the ship's heavy insulation muffled the sound of the crash. No one was in sight or close enough to hear the commotion and investigate its source.

She pulled the revolver from its holster. She had no idea how to use it, but she hoped she would look properly intimidating holding it, thus convincing anyone she encountered on the way to let her pass.

It didn't take long. The Eternity Engine was located midships on the lowest deck.

Greta gasped at the sight of the man she'd traveled halfway across the continent to find. Kit stood near the engine, dressed in the new clothes the Snow Queen had provided. Brown twill slacks were held up by suspenders over a fine white shirt, the sleeves rolled up in his usual manner. He was wearing his spare spectacles, the ones he'd modified to add a variety of magnifying glasses for delicate work.

She slowly approached him as he bent to pick up a wrench from a polished wooden box full of tools. After all this time, she wasn't sure how he would react to seeing her. The words of Elias Hamm and Isadora Halfacre echoed in her mind.

"He seemed smitten."

"Many men have fallen prey to her deceit."

Had her Kit fallen in love with a beautiful monster?

It didn't matter. She was going to rescue him, whether he liked it or not. "Kit!" she cried, shoving the revolver back into its holster. "It's me! We have to get out of here."

Kit turned and gave her the dull stare he'd worn in the townhouse. This close, she could see his eyes held no recognition. Instead, they shone with an alchemical enchantment, turning them from brown to a glittering green.

"Who are you?" His voice was cold as ice. "I'm beginning to understand why Evelyn's other mechanics made so little progress, if they had to deal with this many interruptions. First that odd little man who insisted Miss Derringer had requested my presence, and now this. Whatever it is you need, I can't help. The engine is nearly complete. If I hadn't gone on that wild goose chase the other fellow sent me on, I would have it done by now. Leave me to my work."

Greta stood stunned. What had that monster done to Kit? All the life from his face, his voice and his manner had been erased. He sounded more like a 'gen than the poor butler in the Snow Queen's townhouse had. Now she knew what was worse than trying to turn machines into living creatures: turning a living man into a machine.

She'd come all this way, and, if she couldn't

break that enchantment, she still couldn't save him. But she'd die trying.

She beat her fists against his chest, yelling at him.

"You have to listen to me! She's going to kill you, Kit! She's already tried to kill me. And you're both going to kill a lot more people if you get this infernal machine of hers working." She flung her arms around him, crying into his shoulder.

❄ ❄ ❄

Kit felt a painful twisting in his heart and a stabbing in his brain. He imagined a wild animal caught in a trap, unsure whether to gnaw off its own foot or resign itself to death. He struggled, fighting through the pain to remember this girl. To remember himself. She looked up at him, her green eyes glittering with tears.

His mind recalled the shining ice palace, and the woman he could never quite catch. He'd thought it must be Evelyn, but now he wasn't so certain. This girl's voice felt familiar, like the voice that echoed in his dreams.

"I think you loved me." She pulled a ring out of her pocket, twisting it to play its melody and slipping it onto her finger. "You tried to give me this, but I was too stubborn to listen. I'm so sorry, Kit. I love you. I love you so much I chased you all the way from Missouri."

The feelings of fear and failure, of loss and

longing intensified, but now he could remember their source. The thing he had needed so desperately to finish wasn't Evelyn's machine. It was this — this conversation, with this woman. He had set out to rescue her, but somehow he'd ended up in danger and she'd come to his rescue instead.

Light broke through the fog in Kit's mind. A warm flame ignited in his chest, burning away the icy stabbing in his heart. A rush of memories and emotions threatened to overwhelm him. He staggered on his feet, and the girl wrapped her arms around him again, trying to hold him up.

She swiped the tears from her eyes with the sleeve of her blouse. "I know I never listened to you, but I promise I'll start if you'll just listen to me now."

"But, Greta, you never keep your promises, either."

Even though he felt very groggy, the faint ghost of his usual teasing tone had returned. He stood up straighter and wrapped his arms around her. Instead of alchemical enchantment, his eyes glowed with affection as he smiled at her.

"Are you back? Is it you?" she cried.

"Was I someone else for a while?" He shook his head, still a little confused. "Actually, now that I think of it, I believe I might have been someone else there for a bit."

The events of the past two days clicked rapidly

through Kit's restored mind. He looked at the Eternity Engine and at Greta. Much as he wanted to spend the next few hours expounding on her declaration of love, he knew they were in terrible trouble.

"You know how you promised to listen to me? I need to you do it right now. Hide behind those crates. Stay there, don't make a sound. I can get us out of this, but you need to trust me."

❆ ❆ ❆

Greta looked doubtfully at Kit. He was a mindless machine just a moment ago, and now he was giving orders? On second thought, if she'd listened to him two days ago, maybe none of this would have happened.

She hid behind the crates, waiting.

She was about to call out to Kit and ask him what he had planned, when she heard the clicking of high heels. A woman who could only be the Snow Queen entered, splendidly arrayed in a beautiful bustled gown and dripping with diamonds.

"So we're finally ready to test the machine, my dear?" she purred.

Kit covered a puzzled frown, "Yes of course. You may use it whenever you're ready." He opened the door at the front of the Engine, with a gallant gesture.

He stepped away from the machine and the Snow Queen smiled in satisfaction, running a hand across his face. "Perfect! In just a moment, I'll be as young as you are."

As the woman's hand caressed Kit's face, Greta nearly leapt over the crates. With extreme difficulty, she settled back down.

The heiress glided over to the large cabinet, made of polished brass and glass. Greta shivered as she remembered the similar cabinets in the woman's laboratory, filled with the frozen forms of her victims. She wondered if the Halfacres had managed to reach Mr. Simms, and if the Guild would be able to help them.

The Snow Queen swept her shimmering skirts into the cabinet. From the safety of the shadows, Greta could see the woman's face framed in the round window of the cabinet door as she called to Kit to activate the engine.

He turned and grabbed a wrench from his toolbox, and bashed the door handle of the cabinet so it wouldn't open.

"What are you doing, you fool!" Greta could hear the outraged woman yell, despite the heavy wood and thick glass surrounding her.

As soon as the door latched, a switch had silently fallen at the side of the machine. A moment later the engine fired up, but it made a terrible groaning sound. Cogs and gears clattered in protest as the machine was clearly not operating as intended.

A look of alarm crossed Kit's face. "What

happened? It wasn't designed to do this! The machine wasn't finished." Moving quickly, he tried to throw the switch back, but it refused to move. He grabbed his wrench and bashed it against the switch, but it still refused to budge

Greta watched in mute horror as the glass of the cabinet fogged with frost.

The Snow Queen beat against the glass, her face contorted with rage. She continued to scream at Kit from within the cabinet, but her words were lost to the shrieking of the engine.

He smashed the wrench against the door handle, but it was no use. A layer of ice swiftly glazed the cabinet door, and began coating the wrench. Kit dropped it before the ice reached his hands.

Inside the porthole window, Evelyn's face became whiter. Frost decorated her eyelashes and her lips turned blue. In less time than it takes to draw a breath, she stilled, frozen solid.

Just as she'd wanted, the Snow Queen would never grow old.

Kit ran to Greta, grabbed her by the arm and dragged her towards the door.

"What's the hurry? She's dead! She can't hurt us." She huffed, out of breath.

"I didn't have time to finish the machine, and I didn't turn it on. Someone else must have sabotaged it while I was out of the room, just before you got here. Judging by the sound, we may have just a few minutes before it blows this entire airship to Kingdom Come. There's no time for me to figure out how to fix it. So I really hope you have a means of escape handy?"

"Wouldn't that have been a better question to ask before you rigged an airship hundreds of feet in the air to explode?"

"I'm telling you, I didn't do this!"

"I know. It's just nice to not be the one responsible for an explosion for once."

"That's hilarious. But could we joke about it some other time? For example, once we're off this flying time bomb? I assume you got here somehow."

"This way!" Greta bolted into the lead, her boots thudding against the floor as she steered them towards the docking bay. She hoped the reindeer would carry them both. She hadn't really thought that far ahead.

Perhaps Kit had a point. Maybe planning did have some advantages.

"By the way, I know this is hardly the time, but can I assume you wearing the ring means you've accepted my proposal?" He shouted as a series of troubling loud pops and crackles echoed down the empty corridor. "The proposal you interrupted? In the event we die in a fiery explosion, I'd just like to know before I go."

"Yes, Kit, of course I'll marry you! Assuming we don't both die horribly in the next ten minutes!" They swept past one still, silent 'gen after another, each one a sentinel paying mute tribute to their mistress' passing.

They raced around the corner into the docking bay. The battered reindeer was right where she'd left it, floating nearly a foot off the floor.

"Hey, isn't that from my workshop? You got the featherfall to work?"

She righted it and straddled it. "Yes. I'm sorry about the sleigh."

"What happened to the sleigh?" He climbed aboard behind her, wrapping his arms tightly around her.

"Um, we can talk about it later. Flying time bomb and all that. Hang on!"

She pulled her goggles down, and yanked the ripcord. The second batch of rockets fired to life, and the reindeer shot forward out the docking bay. Greta clutched the neck of the reindeer, leaning as far forward as she could manage. Kit pressed up against her back, and reached up to grip one of the machine's antlers.

A terrible explosion rocked the ship as they cleared the docking bay doors, bathing them in heat. They were only a hundred yards away when they looked back to see the gondola engulfed in flames. It would reach the balloon soon. Like the destruction of Greta's laboratory, there would likely be little debris left when all was said and done.

They had traveled a surprising distance by the time the balloon caught fire. Kit shouted over the wind and the muffled sounds of destruction.

"I must say, I do like this new mode of attire you've taken up. Although I doubt your parents would approve. It's quite flattering, and eminently practical." He pulled her close, as if determined to never let go.

Greta would have flushed even if she was not flying at tremendous speed with no wind protection. "Thank you," she shouted back. "That reminds me, we have to make a detour through Tennessee. I'll explain when we land. I have some friends who promised to provide us with transportation back home."

"Will those friends know where we might find a parson?"

"Hard to say. They live somewhat at odds with convention."

"There are sure to be questions once we return. If we arrive as man and wife, we can tell everyone our absence was because we eloped."

Greta twisted around as best she could, and kissed Kit soundly. The reindeer dipped precipitously towards the ground and she reluctantly pulled away. After they'd righted the reindeer, she shouted back again, troubled by another thought.

"What about the Snow Queen? What will we tell people?"

"Nothing! The press will assume her latest experiment took a poor turn."

"Why, Kit!" declared Greta. "I could learn to like this planning of yours, after all."

CPSIA information can be obtained at www.ICGtesting.com
Printed in the USA
LVOW04s1331110315

430133LV00001B/55/P